LEAVING NORTH HAVEN

Center Point
Large Print

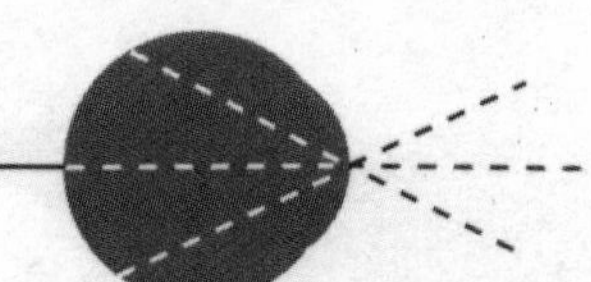

This Large Print Book carries the Seal of Approval of N.A.V.H.

Leaving North Haven

The Further Adventures of a Small Town Pastor

MICHAEL L. LINDVALL

Center Point Publishing
Thorndike, Maine

For Terri, Madeline, Benjamin, and Grace, whose love illumines the way

This Center Point Large Print edition is published in the year 2007 by arrangement with The Crossroad Publishing Company.

The text of this Large Print edition is unabridged. In other aspects, this book may vary from the original edition. Printed in Thailand. Set in 16-point Times New Roman type.

ISBN: 1-58547-903-9
ISBN 13: 978-1-58547-903-0

Library of Congress Cataloging-in-Publication Data

Lindvall, Michael L., 1947-
Leaving North Haven : the further adventures of a small-town pastor / Michael L. Lindvall.--
Center Point large print ed.
p. cm.
ISBN-13: 978-1-58547-903-0 (lib. bdg. : alk. paper)
1. Minnesota--Fiction. 2. Clergy--Fiction. 3. Large type books. I. Title.

PS3562.I51266L43 2007
813'.54--dc22

2006025322

Not where the wheeling systems darken,
And our benumbed conceiving soars!—
The drift of pinions, would we harken,
beats at our own clay-shuttered doors.

—Francis Thompson

The Lord will keep your going out and your coming in
from this time on and forever more.

—Psalm 121:8 NRSV

Contents

A Word from the Author

If I wish to tell you the truth, I might either tell you a story in which truth is incarnated, or I might compress that truth into concepts and abstract ideas that are the other side of narrative. Both kinds of truth telling have their place. I have chosen the former in these pages. The individual tales and the larger story they form in the pages that follow are fiction. Yet fiction is always cloth woven of the threads of real-life stories. Some of these threads are from my experience; others have been related to me. I would offer both appreciation and apologies to all who might see themselves somewhere in these pages, as well as all who have ever told me a tale, some of which has wiggled its way into these narratives. Again, I hope that I have managed to make up stories that tell the truth half as well as life itself does.

Michael L. Lindvall

— 1 —

October 31, All Saints' Day Eve

New Steeple

His lightnings lighten the world;
the earth sees and trembles.
—Psalm 97:4

The last morning of October awoke breathless. Impossibly large flakes of snow, wet and heavy, seemed self-propelled in their headlong descent to the bare earth. I watched them melt almost instantly as they landed on the narrow patch of grass in front of the church. The church lawn is a four-foot strip of sometimes green that lies between the row of insulating hay bales lined up against the foundation of the building and the broken curbing of Jefferson Street. The earth was not yet frozen, but still soft, saturated by a week of cold October rain that had at last become the snow fit for the season.

As I walked to the side door of the church, I saw that flakes were landing in the set of truck tire tracks that sliced deep across the narrow ribbon of the church lawn like a pair of muddy scars. These ruts were the only obvious remaining evidence of the repair work that had followed the explosion of the steeple early in the summer. They had been left by the same tandem trailer that had broken the old curbing as the driver slowly backed his rig up to the church a month ago. The front of the trailer had held a crane that loomed over a reclining steeple, a new glossy-white prefabricated aluminum steeple chained horizontally to the rear of the same trailer. The crane had lifted it upright and then dangled it in the air for some hours like a trophy fish that had finished fighting. Finally it was fitted onto the top of the squat tower at the corner of the church and bolted in place for something shy of eternity.

Four months ago, the third week of June, our church tower had been truncated by what an insurance adjuster from St. Paul had named (under his breath, of course) "an act of God." I do not know how theologically minded insurance adjusters are, but I would guess that they know no more about acts of God than the rest of us. As the pastor of Second Presbyterian Church, I take no responsibilities for acts of God. Yet even in an age that fancies itself free of superstition, people cannot but pause when a church is struck by lightning. Our steeple fairly exploded when it was hit during the peak of one of those dark-as-night late afternoon thunderstorms that rise in the west with the summer heat and rumble east across the prairie. Splinters of pine clapboard and shards of asphalt shingle rained down that 24th day of June, covering the gravel parking lot and the hood of my Taurus. Local Swedes still remember the 24th of June as Midsummer's Day, six months either side of Christmas and midwinter. It's also the feast day of John the Baptist, prophet of hellfire.

I had just parked my car after returning from a trip to Lutheran Hospital in Mankato to visit Minnie MacDowell, who is truly ill at last. It was late afternoon and black as night. I had dashed through a wall of rain and up the wooden steps to the church's side door. Had I walked and not run, I might have actually seen the lightning strike. As it was, I had just come through the door as it hit. I heard it, though it would be truer to say that I felt it as much as heard it. I grabbed a door frame and blurted out to no one, "Good God!" Presbyterian ministers seldom talk that way. I turned to the window that overlooks the parking lot just in time to see a shower of shingles wafting from sky to earth.

The steeple of Second Presbyterian had always been too short. It was designed that way by an architect who had been told by a committee of pragmatic church fathers to make it lower than the town's water tower, which is itself not especially tall. Their theory was that lightning would hit the water tower and not the steeple of the church. It seemed a prudent plan, and for the next 103 years lightning often struck the water tower, which was full of water after all, and well grounded. Lightning had never once chosen the church, not until late last June.

Whispered intimations of providence, or at least an eyebrow questioningly raised, are unavoidable when a church is struck by lightning. Such whispers were amplified by the ironic words that the sign in front of the church had displayed the day of the lightning strike. Every week, in movable white metal letters behind a glass door, this sign announces the title of the next Sunday's sermon. That week they had boldly proclaimed I was planning to preach on the subject of "The Will of God." Bud Jennerson, the editor, reporter, and photographer for the town's weekly, the *North Haven Herald*, had been able to squeeze both the sign with the sermon title and the empty air where the steeple had been into one photo. He had to stand across the street just inside the door of the Two Sisters' Café to do it. He ran the photo on the front page over a long story that ended with a quotation from me. In an interview conducted in a parking lot amid puddles and shingles, he had put the obvious question to the minister, "David, what about lightning and, well, the will of God?"

I had answered and he had quoted, "Bud, I don't know what I know about the will of God."

Come that next Sunday I preached on the will of God nevertheless. It is a topic about which I understand rather less than I had once thought. In that sermon, I rather too deftly distinguished divine will from meteorological phenomena and concluded the sermon standing in an untidy pile of clichés about "mystery" and "moving ahead." I confessed that perhaps you dare not be too confident about any movement of divine purpose until you have come to occupy the high ground of time and are able to look back down at where you have been. This, indeed, may summarize the better part of the wisdom on the subject. My doors are as clay-shuttered as anyone's, and I will have to listen hard if ever I am to hear the beat of any angel wings.

The new steeple is just a bit shorter than the old one. For all its speculation about "acts of God," the insurance company paid up promptly, but not enough. "That steeple was 103 years old, full of dry rot," the adjuster noted. "It's depreciated, you know." The settlement was too modest to re-create the wooden frame structure that had done its unassuming best to grace the church for a century. But the settlement was just enough to purchase and install a prefabricated aluminum steeple. After some summer evenings of Internet research, Elder Bob Beener had requested a copy of the summer steeple catalog of the Aluminspire Corporation of Canton, Ohio. In July, he dropped it off for me to peruse—fourteen pages with color photos, testimonials from other once steeple-less congregations, and a price list.

The six members of the session immediately determined that this was far too delicate a decision to be made by that church board alone and called a congregational meeting to invite a recommendation. At that warm late-August meeting we hung blankets over the windows of the Fellowship Hall so that the pages of the Aluminspire catalogue could be projected on the back wall with an opaque projector borrowed from the elementary school. There followed an hour and a half of debate. Whenever talk turned to wooden steeples, it was punctuated by sober reminders from Bob about the amount of the insurance company's check. Not replacing the old steeple with a new wooden one seemed to many like an aesthetic, even moral, retreat before the relentless press of modern banality, but there was just no money to do it. In the end, the congregation reluctantly chose the Aluminspire "Salisbury 1400" model over the "Winchester Deluxe 1600." The vote was eighty-two to thirty-one with two abstentions. Thirty-three purists, God love them, held out for wood in the face of fiscal reality and simple practicality.

This Halloween morning's wet snow is the leading edge of our tenth winter in North Haven, Minnesota. North Haven lies a mile from the Cottonwood River, south of the Minnesota River, north of I-90, an hour west of Mankato, and two hours southwest of Minneapolis-St. Paul, "the Cities" to everyone, as if there were no others. Even after a decade, my wife and I and our two children, well enough loved though we may be, are hardly counted natives. We came here fresh out of seminary. I was well older than the average seminary graduate. My dossier could not help but betray that I was seven years an undergraduate and that there were several years unaccounted for between graduation from college and the beginning of seminary. These were years too complex and important to be condensed to the three cramped lines provided on the form. North Haven was a singularly unlikely place for us to end up. Annie, my wife, grew up in Terre Haute and Indianapolis. I was raised in a string of generic suburbs, finally being settled for my high school years in a tired little town on the exurban fringes of Pittsburgh. These places passed through my childhood and youth in a sequence I now sometimes confuse. We moved every three or four years as the career of my middle-level management father advanced more or less upwardly. Annie and I came to North Haven largely because it was the first place that would have me, and we needed the job. But we also came partly because we were possessed of an urban arrogance that assumed we could bring something to "these people." We came also because we were romanced by that sentimental vision of small-town life that even my generation still harbors in its imagination.

What we found was less than we had fancied and more than we had dreamed. The town has two hundred fewer souls than the day we came. If it is romantic, it is only so in the way of dying things. The Lyric Odeon Theatre, the town's one notable architectural landmark, no longer shows movies on a regular basis. Karl Sjoberg, who ran it at a modest loss for the last twenty years, died last spring. Now we have to drive to Mankato to the movies or rent videos at the Skelly station. More than half the storefronts on Main Street are darkened voids. Store windows that once displayed coffee percolators, chain saws, and little girls' dresses for sale are now cheered by faded posters announcing last summer's County Fair in New Ulm or displays of local crafts. The *Ojos de Dios*—"Eyes of God"—that Ardis Wilcox's Girl Scout troop made two years ago still stare in a long row from the front windows of the old Woolworth's store. There is a yard between each of them and their red yarn is bleached pink.

Without comment, the *Ojos de Dios* watch Main Street in its languid slide. It is a common enough tale in the little towns on the plains. These are places founded in the grand hopes of an expansive and optimistic age. But good roads, modern farm machinery, dismal crop prices, and the Wal-Mart economy of scale have proven unkind to the dreams of the last century. The rich land yields as bountifully as it ever did, but it simply takes fewer people to coax that bounty forth and get it to market. So like a rising tide, the prairie advances to reclaim what we took from her barely a century ago. Prairie laps relentlessly at the edges of the archipelago of humanity sprinkled ever more thinly across the plains. Most every year somewhere near town, yet another roof of an abandoned farmhouse collapses under a wet spring snow. The windbreaks of green ash planted in the twenties are dying and nobody is replanting them. Long grass grows tall again on what was cultivated land for but a thin slice of eternity.

All this we have come to understand, to love and lament at the same time. Imperceptible decline struck me again on this crisp Halloween morning as I turned on the electric heater in my office. The property committee always postpones starting up the furnace until the last possible autumnal moment. I took off my jacket and sat at my old oak teacher's desk. There were two "While You Were Out" notes set next to each other informing me of phone calls that Maureen, our part-time church secretary, had taken yesterday. The first was from Angus MacDowell saying that Minnie was feeling better and would welcome a visit. Minnie is slipping courageously into the latter stages of Parkinson's disease and had been hospitalized for weeks with a broken elbow. Jimmy Wilcox had also phoned to say that he would be over to fire up the furnace late in the afternoon. "Be sure to leave the back door unlocked," Maureen had reminded me. She also wanted to know which tune I preferred for the middle hymn on Sunday. The organist wanted to know. "The Lord Is My Shepherd" is set to three tunes, each sweeter than the other two.

She ought to know after all these years, I muttered to myself. I always choose "Crimmond."

Ten years is much longer than we had ever planned to stay. A good stay in one place was a gift I was not given when I was growing up. Perhaps it is the memory of those moves from one suburb to another that I suffered in adolescence that has kept us here so long. But we cannot stay forever—not even for a lifetime. It will be hard to leave, almost as impossible to leave as it would be to stay. This decade and the cast of characters with whom we have played it out have proved a subtle drama, a play that demands a close watching. Unless you listen hard, you miss the best lines.

We have discovered that people here are like people everywhere: stiff-necked for no good reason, and kind, even noble, for no evident reason save grace. We have come to know that the movements of life are more easily observed in a small place. When there are fewer things to watch, you watch them all the more intently. You see more in them than you would have ever guessed was there. In the light and dark, the days and nights that would have once seemed uneventful, you sometimes glimpse the shadow of something that may be Purpose, sometimes darting, sometimes lumbering, too quick, too slow for the eye. In the unfolding hands of things that happen, once and again the Secret Thing is held there, and it can be seen sometimes, if you only hold your breath and tiptoe. In these last ten years, I have come to know that I know less than I once did, but I do know this, just this: to see anything that matters, you must always bring two things to your looking—attention, and love.

— 2 —

November 4

Ghost Outfit

. . . we walk by faith, not by sight.
—2 Corinthians 5:7

Minnie MacDowell's summer stay in the hospital the week the steeple was struck had been to nurse a broken elbow suffered in a fall she took in the living room of her own house. The villain, she had noted, was the overly long fringe of her father's old oriental carpet. Her hospitalization led to an overdue and emphatic reconfirmation of an illness she is loathe to confess. This reticence is ironic, since she has been planning on some terminal illness for nearly ten years, ever since she marked her seventy-eighth birthday. This age was not arbitrary. It was, she had read in the *Minneapolis Star* and *Tribune*, the average age of longevity for women in the state of Minnesota. But she had always planned on a straight-to-the-point kind of terminal illness, not one so slow about it. Minnie has spent her entire life doing everything in a deliberate and orderly manner. Her home is orderly; her days are deliberate. Her collection of generic Piggly Wiggly spices is alphabetized from "allspice" to "white pepper" ("black pepper" is to the right of "allspice" under the *b*'s). If she had anything to say about it, her end would be equally deliberate and orderly.

I have been called to her deathbed three times in my years in North Haven. On all three visits I have been greeted by the same scene: Minnie in the four-poster in the upstairs bedroom that she and Angus have shared for nearly seventy years, Minnie in a fresh nightgown with a Bible in her lap, Minnie wearing a deliberately irenic smile. She would languidly request that I read the Twenty-third Psalm and offer the Lord's Prayer. But this I was not to do until after I had asked her "the question." At my first visit to this stage set, I had been gently instructed by Angus to ask her that question needful for any orderly and proper death: "Are you prepared to die?" As the script had it, Minnie would answer "yes," I would read the psalm, we would pray, she would take Angus's hand, close her eyes, turn her head discreetly to the window, and pass away. We had done it all several times, except for the very last part, of course. Three times now, Minnie has lived to die another day.

The MacDowell house is one of several large Victorians that grace Monroe Street, all built at the turn of the century by merchants who had wrestled their modest fortunes from prairie commerce. I recently learned that such homes had once been brightly painted in daring colors we hardly associate with that putatively dour, black and white age. "Polychromatic" was the word the graduate student in architectural history from the University of Minnesota had used when he passed through town. I encountered him standing on the sidewalk taking early morning photos of the MacDowell place. He said he was taking pictures of Victorian homes in small towns in the southern third of the state to supplement his doctoral dissertation tentatively entitled: "Palaces on the Plains: The History of Late-Victorian Domestic Architecture in the Minnesota River Valley." All six of the formerly polychromatic palaces on the plain that line our Monroe Street are now painted white.

When I knocked on the front door for this day-after-Halloween call, Angus greeted me at the door wearing a light gray cardigan over a wool plaid shirt. The outlines of the suspenders supporting his baggy wool trousers were traced under the thin weave of the sweater. Every button was buttoned. It was too tight, even for Angus's bony frame.

"Angus," I said handing him my ski jacket, "you know your house used to be polychromatic?"

He screwed up his face, gave me a dark look, and answered, "Poly what? Don't sound legal, Pastor, not moral neither."

He held my eye for a moment and then slapped me on the upper arm and said, "Ya, ya, I know. It was light yellow and blue with a sort crimson on the gingerbread. Musta looked pretty fancy."

"You ever thought of goin' back to those colors?" I asked.

"Nah," he replied. "White is simpler. White is cheap. What would the town say if the MacDowells tarted their house up? Sure would put the pressure on everybody else on the block, though, that's for sure." I think the latter possibility intrigued him more than a little. "Minnie's back in the sunroom," he added. "She's been sittin' up in a chair the last coupla weeks. The bed was gettin' to her. She'll be glad to see you."

Angus led me through the oversized parlor filled with delicate Victorian furniture pushed up hard against the walls. There were several Queen Anne chairs, a camelback settee covered in a powder blue chintz, and three round-topped tables each crowned with lace and a dozen small, framed photos. In the midst of this heirloom delicacy, a mammoth intruder squatted between two delicate Chippendale end tables. Angus's brown Naugahyde La-Z-Boy recliner looked like a old brown bear snoring between two nervous white-tailed does. I knew that the La-Z-Boy in the living room represented what was perhaps Angus's most notable victory in the decades of give and take in his long marriage to Minnie. Never did I visit that he didn't point to it and say, "Dave, how ya like my La-Z-Boy? Sure is a comfy thing. Minnie don't much care for it. Says it's got no style."

Angus had once revealed to me that he had finally insisted to Minnie that there be one piece of furniture in the house that was his, "sumpin' a guy can actually sit in." After years spent reading the newspaper in an unpadded ladder-back chair pulled up to the kitchen table, he had driven himself over to Mankato and selected the La-Z-Boy. It was brown because the saleswoman told him that brown went with everything. When it arrived, Minnie stared in horror at the interloper lounging in the center of her parlor. "Either that chair goes out the door or I go out the door," she is rumored to have said. But after watching Angus fall asleep in it that evening with the newspaper over his chest, she softened, saying, "Probably would cost a fortune to get the thing back to Mankato." Angus confessed to me that he wasn't actually sleeping that evening, just resting his eyes. He wanted Minnie to see how supremely comfortable the chair was.

The two of them loved each other in the artless way of people who have been side by side for so long that the irregular shapes of their respective beings fit together like two pieces of a jigsaw puzzle. I am sure their love is seldom spoken. But it is palpably real, obvious when you watch them together carefully. Like any holy thing, they sense that it might be diminished if it were spoken of too casually.

Minnie had fallen last June because of her Parkinson's, a disease that had been first diagnosed more than a decade ago. She had scoffed at it for years. Angus never spoke of it. But now there were symptoms that could no longer be ignored, even by Minnie in her silent fortitude. Death she greeted with utter seriousness, but progressive disease she took to be no more than artful malingering. "You have to slow down, Mrs. MacDowell," had been the only counsel of the young gerontologist with a clipboard in his hand. "Take the Sinemet, take it easy, and you might outlive me." This last he had offered with an uneasy laugh. That, of course, was unlikely, but the end of it was that Minnie was not so much terminally ill as she was at last specifically ill. I suspected that there was a part of Minnie that had actually welcomed a prescription for medication as vindication of what she had been telling everybody for years. It did indeed make her earlier retreats to her deathbed more credible.

After Minnie had drifted off to sleep in her hospital bed that afternoon last June, I had taken Angus down to the cafeteria for a cup of coffee. For the first time, he had heard the word "Parkinson's" spoken aloud and in connection with Minnie. It is over such coffee and after such news that people often come suddenly to remember their love and even to speak of it more carelessly than they usually might. I noticed Angus put a finger behind his glasses and rub away what might have been a tear as he stirred sugar into his coffee. Then he had laid the spoon on a paper napkin and said, "Hey Dave, you heard the one 'bout the old Swedish farmer up south of Sleepy Eye?" He let silence sit between us for a moment. "Ya, he loved his wife so much he almost told her."

It was now four months later as I followed Angus past his La-Z-Boy and into the sunroom. It faced properly to the south and, unlike the rest of the dark house, was bright with sunlight reflecting off last night's snow. The weather had turned cold earlier in the week and the big, wet flakes had piled up to a good five inches, not a bad little snow for the first of November. Minnie was not in a nightgown, but dressed in a floral print housecoat. She had no Bible in her lap. This was clearly not to be my last call. As she lifted her hand for me to take, the trembling stopped. It was an almost regal gesture. Had I kissed its back, I doubt she would have commented. Illness and age do make royalty of us.

"How nice of you to come, Reverend Battles. We're glad you could spare the time. We know how busy you are. We—Angus and I," she added, perhaps so I wouldn't mistake her use of the first person plural for the royal "we."

Her smile cracked the Parkinson's mask. We spoke predictably of the two subjects that consume most visits with shut-ins: health and weather. Minnie offered that her health was "fine," which it wasn't, and that the weather, now that the cold rain had changed to snow and the sun was out, was equally "fine." Weather and health exhausted, she took the conversation on a new course. "How about all the kids trick-or-treatin' in the snow again this year," she noted. White Halloweens are hardly worth comment in this corner of the world. There followed a silence as we all replayed in our minds the scene of kids cutting across snow-covered lawns from door to door, not bothering with the shoveled walks.

Angus broke into the quiet. "Minnie had me fish one of the boys' old ghost outfits out of the attic for James. You shoulda seen the kid traipsin' through the snow in a bedsheet. Actually, you could hardly see him. Snow didn't slow him down one bit, though. Not that kid."

Minnie brightened to the topic of James and added, "But it wasn't safe. I made Angus go over to the school and borrow one of the orange reflector belts the crossing guards wear. We put it over the ghost costume so you could see the boy. Running around the way that child does, out in a blizzard in a bedsheet, he was likely to get himself run over."

"It was hardly a blizzard, Minnie," Angus corrected. "But that reflector belt was a good idea."

James Corey is a second-grader who lives across the street and down a few doors with his mother and grandmother. James's mother, Tina Corey, is unmarried and works in housekeeping at the Holiday Inn in Mankato. Tina and her mother had James baptized in our church the Sunday before Christmas seven years ago. Until recently, I had rarely seen any of the three Coreys in church since that memorable day. Tina had carried her child down the aisle alone, her erstwhile boyfriend, the child's father, having fled to basic training. Her plain adolescent face was still pimply. She had trembled with the child in her arms. James had been awake, but quiet, a blue pacifier stuck in his mouth. After I had read the opening part of the baptism service, I came to the awkward question, the one we all dreaded. Our congregation has a tradition in which the minister asks, "Who stands with this child?" The parents and the family are then to stand and remain standing for the rest of the baptism. What we all dreaded was the moment when the only person to stand would be Mildred, Tina's nervous, chain-smoking, little bird-like mother. The scene hurt, a mother so alone, this child so little. But that day when I asked the question, "Who stands with this child?" a most extraordinary thing happened. Mildred Corey stood up of course, but then Angus had unaccountably stood up, though no blood relative to this child. Then Minnie rose haltingly to her feet, and soon before incredulous eyes, the whole church, full that Fourth Sunday in Advent, was standing up with little Jimmy.

He is James now, an extraordinarily active seven-year-old boy who sleeps sporadically, talks without so much as a comma, and moves incessantly. He is a sweet-spirited child, boundlessly enthusiastic about everything. But something is amiss, and were he a suburban seven-year-old, he would doubtless be diagnosed. In his two years at Grant Elementary School, James has exhausted three successive teachers. In fact, his first-grade teacher moved her retirement date up after three months with James Corey. His mother works the eleven-to-seven shift at the Holiday Inn in Mankato and comes home with just enough energy after a day of making up motel beds to put her child to bed. His grandmother manages to get him out the door in the morning, then walks down to the Feed and Grain, where she helps with the books for a few hours, comes home in time for her soap operas, switches to *Oprah* at 4:00, and at 6:45 puts three TV dinners in the oven. Everyone in the little bungalow seems eternally tired, everyone except James, who is never tired.

But providence placed Angus and Minnie on Monroe Street, they having survived two sons of their own now grown and moved away, leaving the big house too quiet and strangely empty of boys. Angus especially has found welcome company in James, the little boy who was quiet the day he was baptized and has been making up for it every day since. The bounty of the child's words easily enough fills the gaps in conversation left by Angus's long silences. Minnie has come to that point in life where the tables of framed photos upset by James, his abuse of china dessert plates, and the toll that his muddy sneakers take on Grandfather Smith's oriental carpet all matter much less than they once did. They both welcome James's unsinkable enthusiasm for everything. They welcome the trail of mittens, boots, hat, and parka that he dumps on the kitchen floor when he comes over to watch after-school television with Angus. Angus and Minnie watch the kitchen wall clock each afternoon, awaiting the sudden din that cuts the quiet of the big old house as James announces his arrival most every weekday at ten after three: "Angus, Minnie, I'm here, I'm here. Where the heck are yous guys?"

Sitting in the bright sunroom, Angus warmed to the telling of his fresh Halloween tale. "James said his mom bought him a Teenage Mutant Ninja Turtle outfit over in Mankato to wear for Halloween," he went on. "But he was real upset about it. Said nobody cares for Teenage Mutant Ninja Turtles no more. Said, 'You'd think my mom would know that.' Said he would die if he had to be a Teenage Mutant Ninja Turtle. So Minnie, she says, 'James, how'd ya like to be a ghost? Our boys used to be ghosts every year for their whole growing-up.' And I say, 'We still got their ghost outfits around here someplace. Probably up in the attic.' "

Angus took up the tale with more enthusiasm than I had seen in him for months. "I found 'em all right. Up in the attic just like I said. Not much to one of Minnie's ghost outfits, just an old sheet cut into a big circle with a couple of holes for the eyes. Then you hold it all in place with a belt around the waist. Pastor, we never held much with this Halloween nonsense. We never paid it much attention when we were kids, but Larry and Donnie said all their friends got to go out and trick-or-treat, so Minnie made 'em these ghost outfits. We kinda kept the whole thing to a minimum, dumb heathen idea if there ever was one, Halloween. Anyhoo, Donnie's ghost outfit fit James just perfect."

"I told Angus to go get the reflector belt when it started to snow," Minnie said for the second time. "Can't see a ghost in a snowstorm," I told him. James was against the reflector belt idea. Said it took away the scariness of the whole thing, but Angus said it was either a safety ghost or a Teenage Mutant Ninja Turtle, take your pick.

Angus had finally sat down next to me on the davenport in the sunroom. Both of us were across from Minnie, who was seated in a chair facing the row of windows, bathed pale in the snow-reflected light. The old man added, "His mom had picked up a plastic jack-o'-lantern bucket for his trick-or-treat loot."

Minnie lifted a trembling hand that stilled as she covered a smile. "The boy was so excited. He couldn't hardly hold still for us to get the outfit on him. He was even more charged up than usual. He was going out to trick-or-treat all alone, so Angus said he would follow behind at a distance, just to keep an eye on him. We called his grandmother and asked if she minded. 'Sure, thanks, keep up with him if you can.' That's how she put it, Pastor."

Minnie asked if I'd like coffee. When I said, "Black with sugar, please," she raised an eyebrow in Angus's direction. Years together make for subtle communication. As Angus rummaged noisily around the kitchen, Minnie leaned over to me and whispered: "Angus'll tell you the next part. Pastor, he's so taken with that boy. Why, James follows him around like a beagle puppy."

She looked toward the kitchen to make sure Angus was out of earshot. Her demeanor and lowered voice suggested a confidential aside. "Pastor, I've known about the Parkinson's for a long time. I remember answering the last letter my brother wrote me before he died. I can tell you just when it was, the summer of '79. I looked at my handwriting, how tiny it had gotten. I had seen in the paper that tiny handwriting is a sign of

Parkinson's. I saw the doctor that fall. He said I was probably right, but for now we'd just keep an eye on it. I decided not to say anything to Angus. It was probably a mistake, but I didn't want to worry him, and the doctor said sometimes it comes on real slow. Pastor," she went on "first I prayed that it would just go away, I prayed that I would be healed of it. Now I don't know what to pray for. I don't know whether to pray for fast or to pray for slow."

Angus returned with an old percolator, the cord dangling over the side of the tray, and three mugs that read "Sleepy Eye Feed and Grain" on the side. Minnie rolled her eyes at this déclassé presentation and reminded her husband that they owned a perfectly good silver tea set and eight sets of bone china cups and saucers. "What are you saving them for anyway?" Angus poured without offering an answer and set about telling the rest of the story, a tale they were obviously both coming to enjoy.

Angus leaned back in the davenport, the coffee mug between his hands. "Well, the kid is so fired up. You'd think he'd never been out trick-or-treatin' before. I get the ghost costume on him as best I can and then I put on the reflector belt. I barely have it buckled up tight when he grabs the plastic jack-o'-lantern bucket and tears out the door lickety-split. I'm tryin' to get into my coat and go to follow him." He interrupted the story for a sip of coffee. "I see him tearing across the front lawn, and just as I step out the door the kid runs full-speed, smack-dab into our big maple. I run over to him fast as I can to see if he’s hurt, but he picks himself up and takes off down across the yard and, would you believe it, he runs smack-dab into the Jennerson’s big box elder tree. Knocks the wind right out of the kid. This time I catch up to him before he gets on his feet again. He’s flat on his back and I look down at him. ‘James!’ I say, ‘Are you okay?’ Then I look close and I see that the eye holes Minnie cut in the ghost costume, they don’t line up with his eyes. Not even close. Kid can’t see a thing! So I reach down and adjust the ghost costume a little to the right so he can see out the holes and he looks up at me, catches his breath, and says, ‘Angus! I didn’t know you were supposed to be able to see!’ ”

They both smiled at the memory of it. “That boy trusts you two,” I said. “You send him out to trick-or-treat blind as a bat, he figures it must be okay. It’s okay if you tell him it’s okay.” Minnie looked at Angus, and Angus looked at his coffee.

As I walked down Maple Street back to the church, I noted the two trees James had collided with, the MacDowells’ maple and Bud Jennerson’s box elder. Stout trees, both of them. I tried to imagine what it would be like to trust anything so utterly as to dash blindly out of the house and down the street.

Such trust haunted me as I walked back to my office ruminating about the next leg of the journey that lay before me and my family. I have spent the last week writing what Presbyterians formally call a PIF, a Personal Information Form, a dossier to the larger world. I don’t know where I am going any more than James did four nights ago. The town has come to be an unlikely home for us, but we can hardly stay forever. The town is withering; the church is withering—neither so much in spirit, but both in numbers. The hard truth is that in a year or two, maybe five on the outside, the church won't be able to pay a minister a full-time salary.

I suppose all of us have our ghost costumes on askew half the time. But as a child trusts an old man from down the street and flies off into the night when he can see nothing before him, we come to trust One who loves us even more steadily. So often what lies before us is hidden. It's either trust and go, or stay in the house. If you stay, there will be neither treats nor tricks, of course. But if you go, you will doubtless run into a tree or two. When you do, all you can do is catch your breath, pick yourself up, and keep going.

— 3 —

November 26

Is This Sausalito?

. . . the kingdom of God is in the midst of you.
—Luke 17:20-21

You might mark the advent of winter here in several ways. Perhaps it's the morning of the first hard freeze, that morning you go out back cradling a coffee mug to warm your hands and find the tomato plants shriveled to black-brown corpses, their skins burst, the red flesh bit white with frost. Maybe it's the first snow that stays the day; the dustings and early flurries of September don't count. But most folks in North Haven count the advent of winter as the day Ollie Lundeen pulls an old wreck of a car out onto the ice of Long Lake just east of town. It's a small lake, not forty acres, and lies along Highway 14 so you can see the wreck as you drive by. The job has been his since the late fifties because he has the only tow truck in town. He doesn't like doing it, even after he's measured the ice in several places to make sure he's got the foot-plus he says he needs to keep him, the GMC, and the wreck out of the water. Gives him the "heebie jeebies," he says. I hear he invariably mentions "heebie jeebies" late every November when one of the members of the Jaycees calls to remind him it's about time to run over to Sleepy Eye and pick up a hulk of a car from Otto's Auto Salvage and pull it out onto the lake. Ollie grumbles, but goes year after year, maybe because he knows winters won't start without him. So winter officially begins the moment Ollie wrestles the hook from the front bumper of the wreck, double-clutches the GMC into second, winces as he hears the gears grind, and creeps off the lake as daintily as you can in a two-ton truck.

The wreck on Long Lake has been the number-two Jaycee fund-raiser since 1957, when Angus told the club about how much money the Rotary up in Willmar was raising with their wreck on Foot Lake. "You sell times," Angus told the Jaycees. "The hour and the day, a buck for each guess. The person what guesses the hour and the day come spring when the wreck goes through the ice, they get half the kitty and the club, they get the other half. It's not exactly gambling. It's just guessin' on the weather, like an act of God."

It's been a real money-maker for the Jaycees these last forty years, second only to the Kaffe Fest. They sell a few hundred guesses. The days and hours and who bought which are marked on a giant calendar that hangs all winter in the Two Sisters' Café. For four months it serves as a poster-board promise that winter won't last forever. The last week of March and the first couple of weeks of April sell out first, of course. Most folks buy more than one guess even though the price has doubled to two bucks. The Jaycees duct-tape a cheap battery-operated wall clock to the steering wheel of the wreck. It quits the moment the car goes under, so there's no quibbling about the exact time. At least there had been no quibbling until this year. They leave a steel cable attached at one end to the frame of the wreck and the other end looped over a fencepost on shore. When the ice is gone, Ollie pulls it out of the water and back to Sleepy Eye. They get a new wreck every year. Everybody says it'd be tacky to use the same one over.

It was the Jaycees' wreck on the ice that finally pushed Larry, the middle Wilcox boy, over the edge. Like both of his brothers, Larry has lived his life at brooding odds with things as they are and the place where he is. Congenital discontent seems to run in the family. Larry's younger brother, Jimmy, has cast himself as the rock of the family—married, albeit laconically, to the same woman, and working, although without passion, at the same job. Larry's older brother, Lamont, got the farm such as it was after his parents moved to Mankato. They had left town as soon as the three boys were out of the house. "Nothin' to do in this burg," was their explanation. Rumor is they don't find much to do in Mankato either.

Lamont spent most of his days as a farmer building a boat in which to sail away from the farm. To the surprise of all, one warm spring day a tractor trailer pulled his home-built sloop out of the barn and all the way to Lake Pepin on the Mississippi. He left the farm to cruise the Caribbean perched in the cockpit, tiller in hand, waving to an incredulous crowd watching silently with their arms crossed in front of them. He's now more or less settled in the Cities. Until this year he'd been back to town but once.

Larry, the quintessential middle child, left town late last spring and much less dramatically. It was all because of the wreck on the ice, people say. Larry was a realtor, in fact the only realtor in a town growing ever smaller with the years. This is a place with an empty house on most every block. Even while he struggled to sell North Haven, Larry's heart, as Wilcox hearts are wont, had wandered elsewhere. Specifically his had wandered to Sausalito, California, just across the Golden Gate Bridge from San Francisco. The office of Wilcox Realty is a quarter of the old Woolworth's store on Main Street. A decade ago, Larry partitioned it off from the unheated vastness of the old five-and-dime. Over the last few years, his fading Polaroid real estate photos of North Haven houses for sale and local stores for lease have gradually yielded their wall space in his office to color posters of Sausalito and maps of the Bay Area.

A year and a half ago now, on a late afternoon in March just before Larry left town, I was on my way home for lunch and happened to glance through his office window at one of those posters. It was a harbor scene, yachts crowded at docks in the foreground, pastel-colored California bungalows climbing the hills of Marin in the background, all soaked in a brilliant sun. I was holding my collar tight against late-November sleet, sharp little ice razors driven by a north wind. The heavy sky was a shade grayer than it had been the day before. Though the big red letters were long gone, you could still read the outline of "F. W. Woolworth" on the storefront above the windows. For forty years those letters had guarded the brick under them from the sun, preserving the deeper, unfaded red. Inside, Larry was leaning back in his swivel chair, feet up on his desk next to a silent black dial telephone. He had a magazine in his hands. He looked up, caught me gazing at the poster, and motioned me to come in. Larry is a member of Second Presbyterian, a semiannual and emergency Christian, single and recently the far side of fifty. That he had postponed marriage until it seemed unlikely was hardly remarkable. Larry Wilcox had lived a life of consummate procrastination.

He sprang from his chair too enthusiastically. I recall

wondering why he should be eager to see me. He bounded toward me. I held out my hand, but he didn't even see it. He pushed the magazine under my nose.

"Look at this," he fairly shouted, slapping the open magazine with the back of his left hand. "Look at this: the average annual temperature in Sausalito is seventy-two degrees! Never gets too hot, hardly ever gets much below sixty. People don't even need heat or air-conditioning."

He put the magazine down and lifted a giant coffee table book off his desk. It was titled *Paradise Found: A Photographic Study of Marin County.* He opened it to one of a dozen pages marked with yellow Post-Its.

"Look, Dave, they have outside restaurants year-around. People are laid-back out there. I mean they don't worry about every little thing like we do. They take it a day at a time in California, you know. 'Whatever,' that's what they always say out there, 'Whatever.' They mind their own business too. Everybody just minds their own damn business. And real estate . . . you wouldn't believe what the business is like."

His eyes and voice were animated by the near religious enthusiasm of a man who had located the Kingdom of God on a map. "Sun shines more in Sausalito than it does in San Francisco," he went on, "and they say the coffee is even better than Seattle."

"Sounds like you're ready to go," I said.

"Oh, eventually," he answered, slapping *Paradise Found* closed. "Eventually," was, of course, the story of Larry Wilcox's life.

But that "eventually" came soon, in fact only a few days later. Larry's leave-taking was less celebrated than his older brother's had been. Indeed, it was much more precipitous. Lamont had departed North Haven after decades of boat-building. Larry left at half past six in the evening the first Friday that April, just after he stormed out of the Jaycees' meeting at the coffee shop, furiously impatient with improbable service club politics. That winter the wreck out on Long Lake had gone through the ice at about one o'clock that afternoon. But it didn't go all the way through the ice, which was the problem that occasioned both the meeting and Larry's leaving.

Ollie had towed a '68 Ford Country Squire out on the lake in early December. A big station wagon encrusted with fake wood and heavy in the rear, she had gone down stern first in ten feet of water. The back end stuck in the mud, the hood and windshield rising up through the ice like a foundering ocean liner. The steering wheel with the kitchen clock duct-taped to it was just above surface . . . and still ticking away. Jimmy said he could see the clock as clear as day with his binoculars. The ethical quandary of the year and the occasion for the emergency meeting was plain to all: does Jasper Werzinski, who had paid good money for the one o'clock, April 4 slot, win the kitty of $434, or do you wait until the clock itself actually sinks? Nothing like this had ever happened before. As a clergyman, I had been called in to render moral perspective. The meeting started over coffee at three. At six thirty, after four pots of coffee and an afternoon of jesuitical moral argument, Larry's younger brother, Jimmy, moved to form a subcommittee to study the matter and bring back a recommendation.

It seems to have been the prospect of a "subcommittee to study the matter" that pulled Larry's eternal "someday in Sausalito" into the moment. He pushed his coffee mug away, stood up shoving the vinyl and chrome chair back across the linoleum floor with a grating scream, and announced, "I'm leaving." Everybody except Jimmy assumed that meant he was going home to heat up a can of mini-raviolis.

But putting his parka on, he announced to the entire coffee shop, "This place is ugly. It's ugly and it's dying. The paint is peeling off half the houses. Kids are moving away. The Piggly Wiggly's gonna close down. It's too damn cold in the winter and too damn hot in the summer and there's nothing to do except gossip about everybody else. And now you're going to appoint some committee to decide if a '68 Ford is really in the lake or not and who gets four hundred bucks." He zipped up the parka, turned to leave, stopped at the door, looked back, and said, "And it's too flat. I'm going to Sausalito."

Jimmy raised his eyebrows and said, "Boy, oh boy." We sat for a moment in silence. Arnie Peterson finally broke the quiet by saying, "Don't s'pose they raise money by putting wrecks out on the ice in Sausalito." More silence as everybody stared into their coffee. Then Arnie smiled wryly and added, "Nope, ice just don't get thick enough."

Larry's Chevy Blazer was heading south on U.S. 71 by 7:30 that evening. Beside him were all his maps of the Bay Area on top of a scant wardrobe of short-sleeved shirts, Bermudas, and blue jeans. This odd detail was noted in the Nebraska Highway Patrol's accident report. Jimmy had showed it to me that next Sunday in my office after church. "Victim subsequently identified as one Lawrence Wilcox, 178 Delaware Avenue, North Haven, Minnesota. Apparently fell asleep while operating vehicle in westbound lane of Interstate 80, seventeen miles west of Grand Island. Vehicle apparently slowed as it left the roadway before striking exit sign for Wood River. Victim unconscious and bleeding from a head wound. Transferred by ambulance to Methodist Hospital in Grand Island." There followed an inventory of personal items in the Blazer with the note about the jumble of summer clothes and maps in the front seat beside him.

It seems Larry had hit the windshield hard enough to send him into a long sleep. After he was transferred to Lutheran Hospital in Mankato, a neurologist named his injury for Jimmy and Lamont one afternoon in May in a flurry of medicalese.

Lamont asked, "What does that mean in English?"

"It means he got bumped real good on the head," the doctor answered. "He may come out of it, probably will in fact, but you never know. And if and when he does, it may, well . . . it may affect him a little."

Larry spent much of the spring in the hospital in Mankato without regaining consciousness. His folks, both in their late seventies, kept watch during the day; Jimmy and Ardis took the evenings. Lamont and his new girlfriend, Tricia, drove down from Minneapolis every other Sunday. All of them came to sit. Nothing much to say or to do, just to be there. They sat faithfully day after day. They sat quietly at first, as you do in the presence of the very ill. But as the reverent weeks became routine, Ardis took to watching her soap operas with the volume low and Lamont and Jimmy, the youngest and the oldest, flanking their middle brother's bed, would talk gas mileage.

I witnessed some of this when I stopped in every week or so. The Wilcox restlessness somehow came to rest in a shared purpose. A reluctant and studiously unspoken family affection hovered in the hospital room. I happened to be just leaving the Saturday afternoon that Larry finally crawled out of his coma. It was the weekend before Memorial Day. Ardis and Jimmy and I were talking about vacation plans. They were going to the Black Hills. The TV was on, suspended from the wall in front of Larry's bed, a muted travelogue no one was watching. No one except Larry. He cleared his throat, opened his eyes, looked at the TV and said, "Is this Sausalito?"

He was moved first to an extended-care facility in Sleepy Eye as he continued to recover from his "real good bump on the head," as his condition came to be named locally. He came home to North Haven a month later. He stayed with Jimmy and Ardis for a few weeks and then moved back into his little house on Delaware.

Jimmy told me that the most curious thing had happened the day he drove his brother home from Sleepy Eye. Larry was sitting in the passenger's seat and intently watching the green high summer landscape roll by. Suddenly he launched into a loquacious wonderment at what he saw. Jimmy noted that they were odd words for a man who had for years spoken with enthusiasm for nothing save Sausalito. It was as though he had never seen that unexceptional stretch of Highway 14 before. He was awed by the size of a stand of cottonwoods near the river. He asked Jimmy to slow down so he could see the corn better. He said the tassels moved like the waves of the sea. Just outside of town, he asked Jimmy to stop the car in front of the old Engstrom place. It's an abandoned farmstead, one of dozens in the county. He opened his door even before the car was stopped and trotted on still wobbly legs up the driveway. Jimmy said that when he got to the end of the overgrown dirt drive, he just stood stock-still in front of the old barn. It has weathered gray and lists to the east away from the prevailing winds. Jimmy said that he stood there for maybe ten minutes and then walked back to the car. "I gotta buy a real camera, Jimmy. It's beautiful, do you see it?" Larry turned and pointed, "That barn is gorgeous."

For the last fifteen months, Larry has done little but take pictures, print film, and mat photographs. Sometimes he takes them in town, but mostly his subjects are old barns and farmhouses on county roads, or rusty hand pumps and windmills that don't work. Many of them are studies of places he once vainly listed for sale. He had even photographed some of them before with his Polaroid, but in the way realtors do. He sees them differently now and photographs them intently, usually in black and white. Often he takes his pictures in the early morning or at dusk. One morning I found him in front of the church with his camera. He told me he likes the mist that sometimes hangs just as dawn breaks. "The light is wonderful," he whispered to me, as if it were a secret he was sharing.

His brothers helped him tear down the partition that separated his office from the rest of the old Woolworth's. He's made the whole place into a cavernous gallery for his photographs. Annie and I went to the much-delayed gallery opening last night. Ardis and Tricia baked cookies. It was cold inside; we had to keep our coats on as the old furnace struggled to keep up with a ten-degree night. Jimmy and Lamont had helped their brother mount track lighting around the room to better show the pictures. There were at least a hundred, familiar places that invited our eyes to see what we had seen so many times, but never quite seen. The pictures seemed to uncover loveliness that we felt embarrassed at having so long looked past. Annie and I bought two, thirty bucks each, mat included.

Larry pulled me aside at the reception to thank me for visiting him in the hospital. He repeats himself, his speech flows to a curious cadence, and he has forgotten the oddest things. He told me that he has shadow memories from the weeks he lay asleep. He remembers people being with him in the room through his long silence, gathered by his bed, two or three voices. He doesn't remember who, but he now knows it was his brothers, guys from Jaycees, some folks from church.

"Same old Larry," he said again, putting his hand on my shoulder just behind my neck and giving me a friendly shake, "except I see stuff I never saw before, stuff that was right here all the time. You know, Reverend, it's not someplace else, what you're looking for. If you can't find it where are, you sure as hell won't find it someplace else."

I watched folks leave with purchases tucked under their arms, small acts of philanthropy meant to be supportive of a brave invalid. Most of them look baffled at having just paid Larry Wilcox good money for a picture of an old barn they drove by every week—in black and white at that. Even Angus and Minnie were there. She's feeling incrementally stronger, but except for a few cautious Sunday forays to church, this was her first outing since the spring. Minnie had a small matted photograph under her arm, now neatly wrapped by a Wilcox brother in brown paper. I had seen her make her selection. An odd choice, I had thought when she asked Angus to lift it off the wall. As he reached for it, I was near enough to hear him say, "Minnie, for goodness sake, it's a thirty-dollar picture of an old wreck of a car out on the ice. Black and white at that."

"Angus, you can't look at it that way," she replied. "It's a picture of one of our traditions. You see a tradition when you look at it. It makes me see it different when I look at it. It makes you think, you know, things right here are worth taking pictures of. And when you do look at it, it's rather lovely."

Angus screwed up his face and said, "Minnie, it's a rusty '72 Cutlass out on the lake. I don't get it."

She had then yanked the photo out of his hands and turned to go pay for it, leaning into her walk with short shuffling steps. It was then that I heard her say to no one, "Maybe he needs a good bump on the head too." She saw that I heard her, turned to me, looked at me with a hint of defiance in her trembling frame, and added, "Pastor, maybe we all need a good bump on the head now and again."

— 4 —

December 12, Advent

Drummer Boys

For we know that in everything,
God works for good . . .
—Romans 8:28

Christmas carols are just that. They are not Advent carols, not pre-Christmas carols, and most decidedly, they are not Thanksgiving carols. That they insinuate themselves into the two months before Christ is ever born is not simply the result of their commercial value as "Sakred Musak" played in shopping malls to induce fiscal indulgence beginning in mid-November. The truth is that we all ache to start singing "Joy to the World, the Lord Is Come" when Mary is only seven months pregnant. We are willing to delay little in the way of gratification.

I said as much, though more discreetly, at the session meeting the first week of December. I noted that we would hardly sing "Jesus Christ Is Risen Today" two Sundays before Easter, though as I made this last point, it did occur to me that the comparison was less than apt. I did not say it, but birth is something you can see coming; pregnancy is sure prophecy. Resurrection, on the other hand, springs up out of nowhere.

Elder Bob Beener had brought up this old and sore subject toward the end of the meeting under the rubric of "new business," though it is clearly very old business. Last year, he reminded the church board, no Christmas carols had been sung at Sunday services until the Third Sunday in Advent, a mere eleven days before Christmas. There had been objections, mostly from the choir, who are hardly purists and have few qualms about singing the praises of "Christ, the newborn King" well before the first contractions set in. Bob pointed out that everybody loves Christmas carols and the congregation sings them well, and with so many of them in the hymnal you need more than a couple of weeks to sing everybody's favorite. And besides, he noted, the Lutherans in town sing Christmas carols all December, the elementary school pageant includes carols, and that event is always the second Saturday of the month. "How can you have a Christmas pageant and not sing Christmas carols, and Christmas pageants always come before Christmas." In the face of such irrefutable logic, the outcome was clear. If I have learned any one thing in a decade of parish ministry, it is to choose battles carefully. This one I counted as no more than a skirmish. Had I pressed, any victory would have been Pyrrhic. I yielded liturgical purity for the peace of the church, both precious, but the latter more so.

Actually the very elementary school pageant that Bob cited as precedent was already much on my mind. Our own two children have graduated from pageantry. Christopher, who suddenly wants to be "Chris," is thirteen and an eighth-grader. Jennifer is eighteen and halfway through her senior year, though she has already graduated, spiritually speaking. They both ride the bus everyday to the Sleepy Eye, North Haven High School having closed its doors in the late seventies, pressed between shriveling enrollment and rising costs. The elementary school pageant had become my concern because James Corey was to be among its *dramatis personae.* James is certainly dramatic enough for any drama, and God gave the child plenty of words. Words overflow James, words about everything, words about nothing. But his many words had become problematic when it came to his proper part in this drama, which, like any drama, is constructed of words carefully chosen by the playwright and necessarily spoken only by the right persons at the right times. James, however, is a verbal geyser; he erupts language whenever stirred by some spirit, a spirit that cares little for the script of some play.

Angus bought me coffee yesterday morning to tell me not only how much better Minnie was feeling, but how worried he was about James and the school Christmas play at Grant Elementary. The child was under threat of removal from the drama for his ill-timed loquaciousness, Angus lamented. Then he asked, "You think there's anything you could do, Dave? You know the teachers over there these days."

The play, Angus told me, had been originally called *The Little Drummer Boy*, but had been changed to *The Little Drummer Boys* when all fourteen boys in grades two and three had indicated on their "Holiday Pageant Sign-up Sheet" that their personal first choice was to be the drummer boy in the play. This character, it was noted, *plays the drum and does not speak any lines,* a dream role for any seven- or eight-year-old boy. Miss Quandt, the new second-grade teacher, is not only in charge of directing *The Little Drummer Boys*, but is herself the author of the work. She immediately recognized the peril of choosing one of the fourteen to be the little drummer boy, and subtly altered the text (*It is my play, after all,* she doubtless said to herself) to make room for a Greek chorus of drums. Miss Quandt also seems to have quickly learned to value peace over liturgical purity. James was one of these drummers, but it was not his drumming that was the problem. I told Angus I would stop by the rehearsal, which he informed me was scheduled for that afternoon, and that I would speak with Miss Quandt.

The peace she thought she had chosen by the politic alteration of her text would be a generous word to describe fourteen little boys with drums about their waists. As I walked into the school's multipurpose room, Miss Quandt was clapping her hands very vigorously to gain the attention of the ring of boys lining the circumference of the room with Wal-Mart toy drums clipped to their belts. These had the look of those ersatz tom-toms with black inner-tube rubber stretched over the top and bottom, the very items that one can find in souvenir shops near Indian reservations north of Brainerd. The boys were drumming loudly and quite independently of one another. Miss Quandt, looking the part of a distracted and frustrated theatrical director, was doing her best to shout over fourteen tom-toms: "Boys, boys, *pa . . . lease* may I have your attention!" Several girls were standing in the center of the room, stifling giggles with hands to their mouths. Others were looking into the room from the corridor, which was obviously serving as the wings for this theater in the round. Boys were drumming at will, just for the joy of making noise. The drums, I later learned, had only just been distributed. I sat down in a folding chair to watch and wait.

The play, of course, had its inspiration in the Christmas carol by the same name. That carol is to my mind an unfortunate piece of music, droning and monotonous, a short, pious "Bolero" without the orchestra or the passion. In the original lyrics, assorted barnyard creatures traditionally thought to be present in the stable at the birth of the Christ child sing in turn, asking what they might bring the Child as a gift. If you can get by singing animals asking rhetorical questions about philanthropy, you come finally to the little drummer boy, whose presence in a stable in the middle of the night is both curious and nonbiblical.

Donkey, sheep, cow, and last of all, the little drummer boy sing the question and then sing the answers. The drummer boy, of course, offers his drumming *(rumpa-pum-pum)* to help the baby Jesus get to sleep. Mary surely loved that. We once possessed a CD called *50 Christmas Favorites* that Jennifer had begged us to order from The Beautiful Music Corporation after she saw their advertisement on television. She was eleven at the time and said she wanted some "real" Christmas music to listen to instead of the "serious" stuff that her parents seemed to prefer. When the real Christmas music arrived in five to seven weeks, it included not only Arthur Godfrey singing "I Saw Mommy Kissing Santa Claus," but also Johnny Cash offering up an inimitable "Little Drummer Boy." She played it again and again that Christmas, until at last I removed it from the CD player when she was on the phone, took it to the back door, and sailed it like a Frisbee over the fence, calling out after it as it disappeared from view, "And a *rumpa-pum-pum* to you."

This being a holiday play rather than a Christmas play, Miss Quandt had thoroughly desanctified whatever sanctity the song had ever boasted of by substituting the phrase "the larger community" for "Him" in her play. This meant that a second-grade girl donkey had to bray out rhetorical questions asking what she might bring "to the larger community." Then, following a moment of reflective silence, she answered her own question. Even though every last soul in North Haven doubtless counts him- or herself as some species of Christian, though some well lapsed and many less than orthodox, the strictures of diversity and political correctness have found their way even to this last outpost of Christendom.

How close the young and generally indulgent Miss Quandt was to the end of her rope I did not know until later that afternoon. This play, I learned, was to be the first public presentation of her prowess as a professional teacher and playwright since completing her student teaching last spring. She was deeply invested in its success. Fourteen little boys with drums could be her early ruin. Several repeated "*pa . . . a . . . lease*s" had at last quieted the drums and the drama began to unfold in all its sentimental earnestness.

If there is any sentiment that James Corey understands, it is earnestness. So when one of his female classmates entered stage right from the hallway and asked, ever so earnestly, what she, a cow, might bring to the larger community, there was no silencing James, who is a bright boy and was simply bursting with good answers to such an obvious question. The child was dancing with answers; his raised hand jabbed the air like a spear, and after keeping his peace as long as he could, he blurted out, "Milk, milk and hamburgers, you could bring milk and hamburgers." He then clasped his hand over his mouth to trap any other errant words from escape. The girl-cow rolled her eyes in the direction of Miss Quandt, slumped her shoulders in mock frustration, and sighed deeply.

Miss Quandt tossed her copy of the script over her shoulder and said, "That's it, James, principal's office, now!" She was near tears, an emotional edge that even seven-year-olds recognize as serious in adults. James marched out of the room in actual tears, his inner-tube drum bobbing wildly on his belt. I rose and told Miss Quandt that I'd follow him down to the office so that she could finish the rehearsal. I sat down next to James in a row of fiberglass chairs that face across the reception counter in the main office. He knows me as Angus's friend and the guy at church in the black dress. Angus has been bringing him to Sunday school for the last few months. He was wiping tears from his eyes and still talking, articulating a reasoned argument that since he knew the answers to all these easy questions in the play, "Why ask them if you don't want answers?" And besides, even in class, Miss Quandt hardly ever called on him when he raised his hand. I, a professional in words, could not even wedge one of mine into a crack in his ceaseless monologue. I began to appreciate Miss Quandt's dilemma.

Later, as Miss Quandt and I sat in the teachers' lounge after the rehearsal (which had gone quite well at last), she explained the obvious. James could not be silenced in the play any more than he could in class. "He talks nonstop, Reverend. Even the other kids avoid him because of it. There is no little switch in his brain to turn the words off. The kid just doesn't have an off switch. I don't know what to do."

What she did do was to sentence James to one day in the principal's office, sitting from eight to two in one of the fiberglass chairs facing across the counter to the desk where Mrs. Lundeen, the school secretary, sits every day from eight to four. Part of Rose Lundeen's job has long been to keep an eye on malefactors like James as they labored in the principal's office through stacks of hellish dittos that insisted dots be connected to form a seal with ball on its nose and others demanding that unlikely pairs of things be matched with connecting lines.

"He'll talk to himself all day," Angus speculated when he told me about James's banishment. The old man had stopped by the church the next morning to see how I had gotten along with my visit to Miss Quandt. "He'll drive Rose nuts by noon, sittin' with her in the office all day, that's for sure."

By eleven, both James and Rose were talking to themselves. Rose had first turned on her desk radio to "golden oldies" to cover James's ceaseless banter: "Dot 38 connects to dot 39 connects to dot 40 connects to dot 41. Hey, Mrs. Lundeen, look at this. It's a seal with a ball on its nose. Have you ever seen a seal? I never have. I saw a seal on TV, but it was swimming in the water and there was no ball. . . ." As it turned out, the radio and James were only double the noise, and by late morning Rose was talking very loudly to herself, if only to concentrate on her typing. The elementary school office has not been much modernized, which suits both Rose, who would have to learn to use a computer if it were, and the school board, which would have to pay for it. Rose's only surrender to modernity was to give up her mimeograph machine for a copy machine. The old switchboard was still behind her desk, complete with plugs and wires that connected callers to one of the eight extension phones in the school. It must have been one of the last in daily use in the Western world.

It was this same ancient switchboard, Rose Lundeen's excitable nature, and James's providential presence in the office that conspired to make the boy not only a minor celebrity, but a hero. Rose herself remembers none of it; James is the lone witness to the events of that late morning. It seems that the phone rang as it had several times that morning, Rose picked it up, answering, "Grant Elementary School, how may I help you?" James's telling and retelling of the story includes an inspired imitation of Rose's saccharine telephone manner. She connected her caller, the custodian's sister calling to ask if he would pick her up on the way home because her car had a dead battery. As Rose was about to turn around to resume her typing, she watched in horror (James mimics her horror by pulling at his hair) as the switchboard connection began to shoot sparks. In another moment, acrid green smoke was pouring from behind the panel, and then flames (which James dramatizes with rapid upward movements of both arms). Rose and James were alone in the office. She yelled for the boy to leave as she walked by both him and the fire extinguisher hanging on the wall toward the washroom down the hallway. There she filled a plastic bucket with water and marched back to the office with James at her heals, who was pointing back to the office and prattling on about the fire extinguisher. Rose threw three gallons of water on the electrical fire in the switchboard, which put out both the fire and Rose.

James's telling this chapter of the tale includes first a series of gestures to convey his impression of electricity traveling from the switchboard to Rose, and then a shaking imitation of Rose electrified, an imitation which would be funnier than it is if it had not been so nearly tragic. At the end of the shaking, he screams and falls flat to the ground and lies still for all of three seconds. He then rises and picks up the rest of the narrative with a self-effacing modesty. He does an in-place version of running to evoke the speed with which he went to get help from Miss Quandt. He next offers a pantomime of Miss Quandt doing CPR accompanied by his own voice-over. If the context permits, he finally lies flat on the ground again, permits a pregnant three seconds of silence, coughs, opens his eyes and groans, "My God, what happened?"

To be both the lone eyewitness to the single most "rad" event to ever transpire in Grant Elementary School, and also to be the hero of the piece has raised

James's profile among his peers to lofty heights. At last the child has something to talk about that someone other that Angus wants to hear. And tell the tale he has—better every time. In class he shares the limelight with Miss Quandt, who is also a hero. He has told the tale in Sunday school; he has told it over and over to Angus, who has yet to tire of it, and he told it to me during coffee hour. I discovered that the child has a sense for gripping narrative, and should he ever turn his verbal skills to paper, he might be a writer. Of course, he would need a strong-willed editor. In his telling of the tale to me and the crowd gathered to hear it at coffee hour, he included both the lying on the floor reenactment and the full catalogue of sound effects. He ended the story by turning to me and asking an honest question about providence.

"Do you think I was meant to be there, Dave?" he asked, raising his eyes and nodding to the ceiling of the Fellowship Hall to indicate the theological dimension of the query.

"Yes, you were," I answered, as if I were any more confident about explicating the purposes of God than I had been when asked not long ago about the sermon I had preached the Sunday after the steeple was struck by lightning. But I was quite sure what James needed to hear. "Mrs. Lundeen sure thinks you were meant to be there." Yet at some level transcendent of my imagination, I have no doubt that a sly old providence had placed James in that office, and good had been worked in this of all things—good both for the child, now a hero, and for Rose, now alive.

Near-death put even Miss Quandt's premier production of *The Little Drummer Boys* into perspective, and when James told her he had a "for sure" way to make certain he wouldn't talk during the play, she agreed to let him back in without even asking him what it was. The night of the play, Annie and I sat next to Angus and Minnie, for whom this was the second evening outing since last June. There were indeed Christmas carols sung, albeit theologically neutered ones. After the kindergartners and first graders finished their medley of holiday songs, Miss Quandt led in her cast, girls in animal outfits and the fourteen drummer boys surrounding the audience.

Annie nudged me, pointed to James, and said, "What in the world?"

I looked at the child aghast and turned to Angus, who anticipated my horror. Without my asking, he answered, "It was his idea, Dave. His and his mother's idea."

Over the kid's mouth was a two-inch piece of clear packing tape. A "for sure" solution indeed. "I rubbed the sticky side of the tape on my trousers a coupla times before he put it on," Angus apologized. "Won't hurt so much when he pulls it off."

It was the sheep who first addressed the assembly, asking, "Bah, bah, what might I bring to the larger community?" James had both hands in his pockets to keep them from raising themselves. There they stayed, however insistently they struggled to be freed. I could see his mouth working through the clear tape, though no sound escaped. It looked like he was trying to say, "Sweaters and lamb chops! Sweaters and lamb chops!"

— 5 —

December 24, Christmas Eve

Homecoming

A man once gave a great banquet, and invited many.
—Luke 14:16

Another Christmas has just slipped from anticipation to memory, where they all lie jumbled together in a pile of sweet sentiment. The more recent ones are spiked with the disappointment that comes with a day that is for adults never what it was for them as children. Deeper in my pile lie memories of my parents when they were young—though they never seemed young to me—remembrances of my mother's grandparents, who descended upon us every Christmas morning in big black Buicks with massive, waist-high chrome grills, memories of long-dead aunties from Pittsburgh who came to Christmas dinner in stout black shoes and forced hard little anise cookies on us, memories of the first Christmas Annie and I kept with a child of our own. This year's Christmas will stand out in the jumble for but one moment, an unscripted word spoken very loudly in the middle of the Christmas Eve Communion Service.

Angus and Minnie MacDowell are stalwarts, not only of the church, but of life in general. Minnie is still reluctant to even say the word "Parkinson's." She just turned eighty-nine and had always imagined a tidier end. Angus, a practiced curmudgeon for most of the century, has grown increasingly careless about that role. He laughs occasionally, rather too often for a credible curmudgeon, and is sometimes recklessly kind. I don't know why this has happened, great age maybe and the enlarged perspective the years so ruthlessly force upon us. Perhaps it's grace, which may be nearly the same thing. Or then again, it may be James.

I have never known a stranger friendship than the one that has grown between James Corey and Angus—Angus, who has made it a life project to speak as seldom as logistically possible and shows enthusiasm for almost nothing, and James, who is a breached dam of words and eager to be distracted by every passing possibility. They are together almost daily. Minnie told me that James is over to their house most every day after school and sometimes hangs around through dinner. Most afternoons at four-thirty, he and Angus watch *The Munsters* together. James dissolves into loud laughter, bouncing up and down in the old ottoman pulled up next to Angus's La-Z-Boy every time Herman guffaws. Angus smiles occasionally, but always with his hand over his mouth. James talks, Minnie says, and Angus listens. But mostly, Angus doesn't yell at the kid, which is unique in the child's experience of adults. He is not an immediately winsome little boy. He's wiry and hard with a round head covered by thin light-brown hair that stands up as if the child were charged with static electricity. His ears stick out and his nose runs ceaselessly. He wipes it once a minute with the sleeve of his sweatshirt. God bless Angus. I don't know if James is a benevolent project for the old man, or just somebody to listen to besides Minnie.

Early last spring, Angus and Minnie had driven to Mankato with James and his grandmother to hear the St. Olaf College Choir sing the Easter portion of Handel's *Messiah.* Minnie told me she had never seen the boy sit so still and be so quiet for so long. They sat at the back of the gym of the state college so somebody could get James out quickly if they had to. But Minnie said he sat on the folding chair, perched up on his knees with his mouth open, his hands limp in front of him like a dog begging. He listened for more than an hour and never wiped his nose once.

St. Olaf Choir cassette tapes were offered for sale in the lobby after the concert. Angus bought him one called *Favorite Sacred Songs.* Minnie says James has about worn it out listening to it on his Sony Walkman. A week or two after that Easter concert, James was a few minutes late arriving at the MacDowells' house after school. Minnie says she pulled back the living room curtains to watch for him and saw the boy standing in a light, cold rain in their front yard, completely motionless, his eyes shut tight, the earphones of the Walkman lost in his disordered hair. He was listening to *Favorite Sacred Songs*. Minnie called for him to come in before he "caught his death a cold." He opened his eyes with a start and looked at her as if he'd been shaken out of a deep sleep. After *The Munsters* were over, he asked Angus where heaven was.

Angus had said he didn't rightly know, but he'd ask the preacher, which he did at coffee hour the next Sunday. I don't recall how I answered, but I remember mentioning that kids James's age often start asking about God. So Angus has been bringing him to Sunday school since last April. Though there were only six weeks of Sunday school left before the summer vacation, the first-grade Sunday school teacher quit the next Sunday. We had even more difficulty than usual finding another one. This interruption had but briefly forestalled James's religious pilgrimage. It did not deter him from Sunday school attendance, nor did it stop him from harassing his mother until she consented to bring him to the eleven o'clock Christmas Eve Communion Service. It seems many of the Favorite Sacred Songs on his cassette tape were Christmas carols.

Angus and Minnie have a lifetime of experience with boys, having had two sons of their own, gone west both of them, and there grown into taciturn middle-aged men. Larry went to Spokane and his younger brother, Donnie, to Southern California. Angus and Minnie have grandchildren, four of them. Larry and Sherry and their three get back to Minnesota to see the folks most every year, usually over the summer. Donnie went to Los Angeles after dropping out of

Mankato State and almost never comes home.

The Tuesday after Thanksgiving, Minnie called and asked if I would stop by on my way home. She had a question about divorce. When I arrived, Angus served coffee—with the silver and bone china this time—but then returned with sugar cubes in one hand and a paper carton of half-and-half in the other. Minnie said nothing. After Angus had retreated to the living room and his La-Z-Boy, Minnie put a series of questions to me about my family and things at church. It was a delay, carefully premeditated and all spoken in a voice that was going flatter and more toneless every time I saw her. The Parkinson's was settling deeper.

We made conversation far too polite and preliminary for people who know each other well. After my answering a question about Jennifer going to college, she seemed at last tired of stalling. She raised her coffee cup to her mouth with two hands. They trembled less when taken from her lap, but even then they were hardly steady. Lukewarm coffee spilled down her yellow housedress. She set the half-empty cup back on its saucer, the two pieces of china rattling a staccato against each other. Her face without a hint of affect, she looked down and suddenly confessed to me that Donnie had gotten a divorce. This was a word she could not utter while looking her pastor in the eyes.

Local sources had already informed me of this, not only the divorce, but also about the custody battle, the alcoholism, and the serial bankruptcies that formed the outline of the Donnie-in-California story. Alvina

Johnson, a wealth of local history, had once told me that it all began with a famous row in the MacDowell's kitchen in 1966 when a long-haired, bell-bottomed Donnie had just told his father he was leaving for California. One observant neighbor estimated that Angus had expended more verbal energy in that one afternoon than he had in many an entire year. Things had long been awkward between this younger son and his parents, but the abysmal nine-month college career and the decision to drop out had been impossible for his father to accept. Thirty-six years ago, he had been not only a younger but a harder Angus.

Minnie told me about the divorce because Donnie had called to say he was coming home for Christmas. He would be coming alone, and she imagined that as a minister, I would wonder where his wife was. I knew that Donnie hadn't seen his parents for nearly a decade but asked carelessly how long it had been since he had been home. Minnie explained his absence to me on the grounds of the separation and the divorce. She told me that most years Bryan, Donnie's nineteen-year-old son, was shuffled back and forth between his mother and father as required by the judge in the joint-custody arrangement, Christmas Eve at one parent's house, Christmas Day at the other. For years, she said, this arrangement had made holiday travel impossible for Donnie. By this mother's logic, some California judge was to blame for her son's long string of holiday absences. She looked at me as she offered this explanation to see if I believed it. She pretended to believe it herself, if only because she had to.

But this year Donnie had called the week before Christmas to say that he was going to close the video store late on the twenty-third and catch the 9:03 Northwest flight to the Cities the next morning, the twenty-fourth. He'd rent a car and should make it to North Haven in time for Christmas Eve dinner. Then he added, "And tell the old man that I may even let him drag me to church." Minnie and Angus fretted over the menu for the homecoming dinner for the next week, struggling to remember whether it was pot roast or meat loaf that Donnie had so favored when he was in high school.

I stopped by late in the morning of Christmas Eve's day to give Angus and Minnie a canister of *Pfeffernuesse* that Annie had baked. Minnie was sitting at the kitchen table directing Angus in the cooking of pot roast. The smell of onions hung like the incense of home in the too-warm kitchen. I couldn't stay and was on my way out when the phone rang. I turned to watch Minnie push herself up from the table and move toward the wall phone as fast as tiny steps could carry her. With sudden life in her voice, I heard her call to Angus who was at my side, "It's Donnie all the way from California." Long-distance telephoning is still a wonder to this generation. It was indeed Donnie calling all the way from California to say he had just missed his flight out of LAX, but Northwest was trying to get him on the 10:23. "Maybe, Mom, maybe not."

Minnie put down the receiver and went to check the

pot roast. Angus opened the front door, and we both looked at the snow that had been piling up all day. We knew it would make Donnie's drive from the Cities to North Haven long and slow. Angus and I looked together at the dining room table. He must have set it yesterday, set it elegantly for three with heavy flatware and fussy china from the thirties, two goblets at each place. All of it wedding gifts, doubtless. The seldom-used stemware had been dusted and the good silver polished by Angus a week ago.

The 10:23 didn't get in to Minneapolis till just after six o'clock. Donnie called from the airport and reported on the snow in the startled way of people who seldom see it. He said he would get there when he got there. Angus and Minnie waited until the last possible moment, beyond the last possible moment, before sitting down together, the two of them at the table set for three. As they ate, I can imagine them listening for their son at the backdoor just as they had listened for him to come home so many nights thirty years ago. At last, they put the leftover pot roast back on the stove, set it on low, put on their coats and black zip-up rubber galoshes, and set out in the Chevy Impala on a three-block drive through the still-falling snow to church. The deacons keep offering to have somebody stop and pick them up, but Angus says, "Nah," and gives his head a quick shake. Recently though, he has taken to adding, "Thanks for the offer."

They were very late when they arrived. The sermon was over and Arlis, our star soprano, was wobbling through "O Holy Night" with a bad cold. As she sang, I parted the red sea of poinsettias to stand behind the old dark-oak communion table to begin the celebration of the sacrament. The church was packed, which it seldom is anymore. Some of the Wilcox cousins from Edina had been so guileless as to sit in the very two places that Angus and Minnie have occupied every Sunday since Herbert Hoover was president.

I turned to the table before me set with two stacks of trays holding round rings of little glass communion cups and silver plates of carefully cubed Wonder Bread. Pinching the little crosses on their tops that serve as handles, I lifted the covers from the top of the round trays holding the rings of little glass shots of Welch's grape juice. Gently, so that no pieces of bread stuck to them, I pulled the linen napkins from the trays filled with cubes of bread. I folded them and lay them next to the tray covers. Such a careful feast, I thought, such orderly flesh and blood.

As Arlis vainly reached for the operatic notes at the end of her solo, I looked down the center aisle to see Angus and Minnie still standing in the narthex. Snow lay unmelted on their shoulders. They looked back up the aisle and into the sanctuary to find their accustomed places taken by strangers come home to be with their families. Angus had his hat in his hand. Even from forty feet away, I could see that Minnie was shaking.

Arlis finished "O Holy Night," sat down, and stifled a sneeze with her handkerchief. I opened my prayer book to the Words of Invitation. I looked at the faces of all the invited seated before me in the darkened church. There were familiar ones and strange ones, all home to keep the feast. I looked back down at the book and began to read, "People will come from east and west and sit at table in the Kingdom of God. Jesus said, 'Come unto me, all you that labor and are heavily laden, and I will give you rest. Whoever comes to me, I will in no wise cast out.' " I had planned to let silence rest in the church for a moment after that last word.

James Corey was in the very front pew with his mother and grandmother. He was wearing a new red Christmas sweater, his unruly hair parted and set in an unnatural order by a generous application of some hair product. Both women had earlier offered me glances meant to apologize for James's behavior during the service. He had been quiet, listening intently to the music, but he would not sit down. Indeed, he had spent the entire first thirty-five minutes of the service on his knees in the front pew looking backward to the rear of the church. And just now he had stood up on the seat of the pew, still facing backward, looking over the heads of the congregation. He was standing up for Angus and Minnie, as they had once stood up for him. As I finished the Words of Invitation, James caught sight of them and began waving his arms like a pair of windshield wipers on high speed. His mother was pulling at the hem of his sweater to coax him down. The silence I had planned held for only a few seconds. As I finished my sober intonation of the words, "Whoever comes to me, I will in no wise cast out," James fairly yelled into the quiet of the church, "Angus! Minnie! We saved a place for you guys for the dinner. We thought you'd never get here. We've been waiting and waiting and waiting."

The child's disruption was hardly worshipful. No one had seen a hint of humor in it, yet it struck me later that night as I sat exhausted in front of the lighted tree in our living room, a glass of merlot in hand, that just as James waited for Angus, just as Angus and Minnie waited for Donnie, there is a Child who is waiting, watching and waiting, just for us.

— 6 —

January 6, The Day of Epiphany

No Heart for It

. . . he did not do many deeds of power there,
because of their unbelief.
—Matthew 13:58

Jimmy Wilcox nearly died the first week of the year. In a sense perhaps he did, and maybe his dying did him some good. Pushing fifty, Jimmy is the youngest of the three Wilcox boys. Lamont, the oldest, sailed off in his home-built sailboat some six years ago. Down the Mississippi he went and into the Caribbean, where the plywood *Lady Barbara* sank in waters too deep for salvage. Lamont is back in Minnesota, taken with a youngish widow from Golden Park named Tricia, and merrily peddling Jet-Skis in Wayzata.

Larry, thoroughly the proverbial middle child, lost himself trying to sell real estate in a town where everybody moves out and nobody moves in. He found himself only after falling asleep at the wheel and running his Chevy Blazer into the Wood River exit sign in central Nebraska. He never made it to Sausalito, but he has made it after a fashion here in North Haven taking artsy black and white photos of rusty old hand pumps in tall prairie grass and sunrise studies of falling-down barns, tilted eastward with the west wind in their slow dereliction. He sees them with great love, he says, and sells more than a few of these stark photos matted in white and framed in chrome through trendy galleries up in the Twin Cities. He sells just a few here in town, mostly to folks who want to be helpful.

Jimmy is the third of the boys but was never the carefree youngest child. For years, he had played the stalwart stay-at-home to his two spiritually and geographically wandering brothers. Though the youngest, he reminds you of the big brother in the Parable of the Prodigal Son. He habitually acts the part of that elder brother, standing by faithfully through sibling wanderings and returns. But even as he stands by faithfully, he does so like the chorus in a Greek tragedy, sighing caution and recrimination from the edge of the stage. Unlike the Prodigal's big brother in the Bible, he never offers any right-to-the-point bitching. Rather, Jimmy's nobly pained expressions and sly critiques of his two brothers are studies in subtlety. In truth I suspect that he has rather enjoyed playing his role as "the dependable Wilcox boy." "Joy" is hardly the word for it, however. You would not be given to include that word very often in the same sentence with Jimmy Wilcox's name.

For many years, his two wayward brothers had unintentionally given Jimmy an identity. Their instability had bequeathed him a place to stand in the world, a piece of ground higher than the only other spot he occupied in life, that of the kid brother who runs the struggling heating and air-conditioning outfit in a small town. So he plays faithfulness in contrast to their unfaithfulness, constancy in the face of their inconsistency. Folks who know the family often rehearse the nautical saga of Lamont or retell the unreal tale of Larry, each story now pressing itself to a quizzically happy ending. When they tell these Wilcox tales over evening beers at the Blue Spruce or morning coffee at the Two Sisters, the telling ends noting that Lamont is happy with Tricia and that Larry sells enough photos to pay the rent. Then the teller offers a stretch of silence offered up to the mystery of providential endings, someone invariably adds the liturgical "amen" to the cautionary tale with the same words: "Well, thank God for good old Jimmy."

But just when Jimmy's two brothers had found their respective ways, Jimmy lost his—at last and serendipitously. With his brothers once lost but now amazingly found, Jimmy had suddenly been robbed of his role as the good son and dependable brother. He was just

Jimmy who sold reconditioned blower motors and window AC units. He was Jimmy who came into the Blue Spruce every Friday night with Ardis and ordered the fried whitefish and ate in silence across from his wife at the same table by the east window. He was Jimmy who always tipped Janice $1.75—a one and three quarters lined up across the top of the bill. He was Jimmy, whose marriage to Ardis was neither happy nor unhappy, just a stack of predictable days piled on top of the one before like a skyscraper of wooden alphabet blocks, getting tippier as it grew taller. They had one adopted child, now a teenaged boy, Jason, whose unhappy story was just about to enter its unhappiest chapter. Now that Jimmy's two jerk brothers had found themselves, this stalwart middle child had no one to play his life off. Jimmy suddenly had no clear idea of who he was or where he was headed. Indeed, he had no clear reason why he was on the trip in the first place.

Churchgoing had always been a part of Jimmy's practiced respectability, so when his and Ardis's spot in the fourth from the last pew on the pulpit side had been empty mahogany for a month running, even on Christmas Eve, I called him and asked if I could buy him a cup of coffee. It was the second week of Advent. There was an almost impolite silence from the telephone for an uncomfortable moment before Jimmy mustered a laconic "Sure, why not?"

We met at the Two Sisters and sat in one of the five booths. The seats are covered in robin's-egg-blue vinyl, repaired here and there with duct tape of a slightly darker blue, a valiant attempt to make the place decent on a budget. Coffee came without having to order: two heavy ceramic mugs and a handful of creamers tossed out like dice onto the worn Formica.

"You and Ardis okay?" I asked Jimmy. "Are you guys upset about something?"

"I dunno," was his first answer. He seemed to be deciding whether to speak or drink coffee with me as I talked. He decided, and said, "Nothing seems to matter, Dave. I mean, what the hell is it for? You hang in there all these years, just tryin' to do the right thing, so what's it all about?"

He stared into the little boomerang shapes molded into the Formica of the tabletop, a sixties design flourish, once modern and daring. Then an image shaped itself in Jimmy's imagination, a picture of his melancholy that he was perhaps borrowing from the wanderings of his prodigal brothers.

"Pastor, I feel like I'm headin' west on I-90," he said, hands surrounding his coffee, looking at me for the first time. "Pontiac's on cruise control, doing a nice steady seventy-five, hands on the wheel at ten and two, just like I was taught. Engine's running okay, heater's on and working, but there's no point to the trip, nowhere to go. Nothing worth looking at out the windows, lots of dirt and snow, nothing interesting, I mean. And it's starting to get dark. And the road is going to Sioux Falls, Sioux Falls, that's where it's going, and hell, who wants to go to Sioux Falls? I mean, Pastor, here I am on the road for fifty years, no exit, no scenery, nothing but billboards and truck stops and then, well . . . Sioux Falls."

Jimmy's foray into the softest edge of profanity—with his pastor no less—was odd for him and every bit as telling as his journey image. A picturesque metaphor for existential despair, I thought to myself. Maybe Jimmy had read Sartre in junior college. No, I answered myself, this is homegrown ennui. I was thinking of a response that would not descend into plastic piety, groping for something to say that went beyond cliché. I almost muttered something about virtue being its own reward, but I'm no longer so sure it always is.

I was saved from easy piety when the midmorning quiet of the Two Sister's Café was suddenly interrupted by a pair of unfamiliar customers. They were struggling with the café's aluminum storm door and second heavy wooden door, a two-door system for keeping cold outside and warm inside that was obviously something of a novelty to these two. Finally, after what appeared to be good-natured jostling, in stumbled two bleary-eyed eighteen- or nineteen-year-olds, one of them in a light windbreaker, the other in nothing more than a sweatshirt and a baseball cap. This, of course, was clothing far too trivial for the fifteen-degree day they had dashed through between their pickup and the door of the Two Sisters. I had noticed it when it pulled up, a black Dodge Dakota with pin-striping down the side and a Louisiana plate. "Sportsman's Paradise," it read. The pair came in hugging themselves against the startlingly cold air, singing a bird-like duet of "burrrr's." The eight

Minnesotans inside didn't need to see the truck's license plates to guess that these were not just a couple of guys from Mankato.

Suspicion was confirmed when the one in the baseball cap called out in a voice too transparently gregarious for rural Minnesota, "Howdy, ma'am, it's colder than a penguin's ass out there. I don't know how y'all take it. Don't s'pose you do grits with your eggs up here?"

Joyce, one of the two sisters and the only waitress on duty, looked innocently mystified and asked, "What's a grit?" The two of them looked at each other, pointed cocked index fingers at each other's chests in perfect sync, and said in unison "What's a grit?"

One of them turned to Joyce and added, "You're the second waitress north of St. Louis who's said that."

They sat down at the counter across from the booth where Jimmy and I were nursing our second cups. They ordered their gritless breakfasts, and as they talked to each other everybody in the diner found a reason to have yet another cup of coffee. We listened to their somewhere-south-of-Iowa accents, carefully feigning disinterest. Haggard as they looked, this pair was obviously having a grand time. Wiping the last of his over-easy eggs with a corner of toast and popping it in his mouth, the one in the windbreaker swiveled around with his coffee cup in his hand, looked at Jimmy and me, and said, "Excuse me, but are y'all from around here?"

It was not a hard question, but both of us hesitated in

the face of such wanton familiarity. "Ya, sure, we live here in town," Jimmy answered.

"Well, me and my buddy are up here on a bet. We live down in Monroe, Louisiana, and last night we were having a couple of cold ones in this place on the edge of town, and well, to make a long story short, Roger's brother-in-law . . ."—he pointed his thumb at Roger, who was finishing his three-egg omelet. "This is my buddy, Roger. Anyway Roger's brother-in-law says to the two of us, 'Three hundred bucks you can't drive to Canada and back in twenty-four hours without going on a single interstate.' Well, this is only our third stop. Never saw snow, not ever in my life, not until this mornin'. Don't never snow in Monroe. It's something to see, you know that? I mean, mile after mile of the stuff, a sure wonder it is."

He paused for a moment to reflect on his own reflectiveness, and then added, "I'm T. J., by the way." He stuck out a hand toward our booth. T. J. was garrulous, certainly by Minnesota standards, but it was clear that his friendliness was leading up to something.

"This mornin' Roger and me were drivin' along, heading north on Highway 4, I guess it was. We were looking out at all that snow trying to stay awake, and out the window on the left-hand side of the road is this big flat field, flat as anywhere in Louisiana, but it's covered with snow and all over the field are these little-bitty houses, I mean the littlest houses you ever did see, little tin chimneys stickin' out of 'em, couple cars parked out there in the field, but no phone wires or nothing. It was the funniest little town I ever laid eyes on. Dirt poor, that's for sure. I mean, I gotta ask, what kind of a town was that? It was maybe twenty miles north of the Iowa line, off to the west in a big field."

Jimmy looked at me, and I at him. We both smiled, the first smile of the morning.

Jimmy answered for us, "That was no field," he said. "That was Cedar Lake all froze over, you know. And the little houses out here, they're ice shanties." This obviously needed interpretation, and he added, "You know, ice shanties. People sit inside of 'em, and you chop yourself a hole there in the ice and sit inside and you go fishing."

T. J.'s eyes narrowed, he licked his lips, and looked toward Roger, who had been listening to this explanation over his shoulder.

They broke out into simultaneous laughter, each swiveling his stool to face the other, and pointing cocked fingers at each other as they roared. "Now that's a good one, ain't it Roger? Little houses on top of froze water. Fishing through little holes in the water."

T. J. swiveled back to Jimmy and smiled, "Bet you thought we'd fall for it. Bet y'all try that one on all the tourists."

They left the Two Sister's Café and climbed into their pickup still shaking their heads, obviously admiring Jimmy's inventiveness, enjoying his cheeky play with a couple of good old boys on the road. "Little houses on frozen water, people inside peerin' down and fishin'." It was a wonder that required the imaginations of two teenagers from Monroe, Louisiana, to stretch beyond the limits of their adolescent elasticity. In utter and wise incredulity they roared north toward Canada.

Jimmy had his heart attack shoveling snow later that week. When I got to the hospital in New Ulm, I found Ardis in the family waiting area outside the emergency room. As I sat down next to her, she tugged on the straps of her vinyl purse and said, "Dave, we may lose him. The doctor said it was a pretty bad one, and even if he makes it, there'll probably be, you know, damage." We went into the E.R. cubicle hand-in-hand. I prayed with Ardis over Jimmy: gray, ventilated, wired, surrounded by what looked like half of a Radio Shack. I prayed for recovery, of course, for what was doubtless a miracle.

Which is exactly what we got. Once and again damaged hearts heal strangely fast and the near-dead seem to rise. To everyone's surprise, Jimmy not only made it, but made it with barely a trace of detectable damage to his attacked heart. I happened to be in Jimmy's room on the cardiac wing when a youngish resident had knocked hesitatingly on the door, entered with a "Hello, I'm Dr. Burrows," and said, "Well, I've got really good news for you, Mr. Wilcox. Your tests are coming back great. I mean, you're probably going to be okay. We can hardly believe it. I've never seen anything like it."

Jimmy's response to news of a miracle was disbelief that such a thing could be. "I wish I could believe it," he said, avoiding my eyes. "I wish I could believe it. I want 'em to run some more tests."

The resident left with a promise to send the head of the cardiology unit in to confirm the test results. We talked, Jimmy and I, and as we did two true things sneaked into the dim light of the sickroom. I saw them first; Jimmy did not see them, at least not until much later. The first was this: Jimmy was afraid to trust anything that looked too good. He always had been. But another thing, even darker, also slid into the room. It hid itself in the corner, but was very much present with us. In the days after his brush with mortality, Jimmy had made his peace with death. And now, death forestalled, the prospect of another thirty years of life give or take, was something he greeted with more anxiety than hope. This sometimes happens when people who aren't supposed to get better do. The ironic truth is that sometimes it takes as much courage to face the prospect of living as it does the alternative.

The head of cardiology was in Jimmy's room an hour later. No hesitant knock at the door this time; he strode in clothed in white-smocked authority, peering at Jimmy's charts through horn-rimmed half glasses and then over them at Jimmy. I thought to myself, "Here is a surgeon from the days before they invented bedside manner."

"I'm Williams," he said to both of us. And then to Jimmy, "Young man, do you know how lucky you are?" "Young man!" I thought to myself. Williams went on, a sixty-five-year-old looking down into the bed of a forty-nine-year-old, "Myocardial infarction of the magnitude that you suffered and you're fine. I have seen things like this a few times in forty years. Can't explain it. Burrows says you don't believe it. Mr. Wilcox, I've spent too much of my life giving people bad news, and when I give people good news, even too good to be true, I expect them to accept it. You're out of here in two days." He was home for Christmas, stunned by another and more personal miracle.

Jimmy and I had coffee again at his place this morning. The Day of Epiphany, the sixth of January, largely ignored by most Protestants, had dawned clear and cold. He had asked me to stop by not because he had much to say to me, but because we never finished our talk a month earlier. I was duty-bound to say the obvious, of course, namely, that by some grace, he had his life back.

"You're on the road again," I told him, remembering the existential highway image he had used on me to draw a picture of his listlessness. "Jimmy, you thought you had exited, but providence routed you right back on I-90 westbound, and Sioux Falls is thirty years away." I remembered the boys on the road from Louisiana who had forestalled the platitudes that I doubtless would have offered about the meaning of life. I remembered what they had seen, but refused to believe possible. "And there are all sorts of sights to see, things too strange to believe. Sometimes they're so delicious you're afraid to taste them. We're always looking for obvious miracles, I mean out-of-nowhere things you can't explain. But usually miracles are something you don't even see at first, just tucked in the routine."

I looked him in the eyes and continued with the sermon I figured he wanted. After all, if you don't want something like a sermon after you've been snatched from death, why invite a preacher for coffee? "Jimmy, you never see the wonders unless you expect to see them there. If you don't expect them, you never see them." A reoccurring and ironic experience slipped to mind. I told Jimmy about it.

"Sometimes Annie and I go up to the Cities, and I'm driving around looking for a place to park on the street downtown. Too cheap to pay for a parking garage. We're in a hurry, of course. Late for dinner or a concert or something. I get so intense about looking for a place to park that I start going too fast, and, all of the sudden, I drive right by an empty spot. And that gets me mad, so I drive faster, and then I go right by another empty spot or two. Then I slow down."

"But how about when you're driving down the highway and it gets too dark to see?" Jimmy asked, staring into his black coffee.

"Well," I stalled, thinking to myself that these motoring metaphors had been stretched beyond their limits, "It gets dark, you turn the headlights on. You can only see as far as the headlights shine, but that's all you need. You get there, you get there even if you can only see one stretch of the road at a time. That's usually all you get to see anyway. You just drive into what you can see in front of you."

"I suppose so," he answered and looked out the window.

— 7 —

February 14

Valentine's Day

> He did not weaken in faith when he considered his own body, which was as good as dead because he was about a hundred years old.
>
> —Romans 4:19

Anna-Lena Wilcox died the second week of February. She was ninety-four and still in good health, though obviously not perfect health, and stubbornly resolute in her good spirits. Anna-Lena was the Wilcox boys' paternal grandmother. She had never lived anywhere but North Haven and had left Minnesota only once to visit California, which she pronounced "nice, if you like that sort of thing." For twenty years, she had lived alone in a sagging little bungalow on West Adams. Larry and Jimmy, her only descendants still in town, took turns looking in on her every few days, which regular attention Anna-Lena dismissed under the general category of "making a fuss." "To make a fuss" is a vaguely pejorative label her generation applies to inappropriate attention paid to problems and people. It's not that Anna-Lena didn't think she deserved Larry's visits on Mondays and Thursdays, plus the ride to church on Sunday from Jimmy and Ardis; she simply didn't think she needed it.

She was a member of that vanishing generation of women, now old ladies, who never drove a car. She walked to the Piggly Wiggly every other Tuesday at nine o'clock sharp pulling an old Radio Flyer wagon that would bear her two bags of groceries the four blocks home. She could have easily walked to church as well, but Jimmy insisted on picking her up. Never once in the last fourteen years did Jimmy open the front door of his car for her on Sunday morning at ten minutes to ten that she didn't shake her head and mutter, "Don't know why yous are makin' such a fuss." Anna-Lena had been a pretty farm girl who spoke little English when she married Lawrence Wilcox in 1924. To the day she died, her sentences rose in tone in the Swedish way as they moved toward a period.

The funeral was on the afternoon of Valentine's Day. It was sparsely attended as services for the very elderly often are. The two dozen of us sang all the verses of "Abide with Me" and filed out of the church and to the cemetery in seven cars, each with a little orange flag supplied by the Schultz Funeral Home in New Ulm secured by a magnet to the roof just above the driver's head. Clearly these orange flags would fit under Anna-Lena's category of "making a fuss." It had turned oddly warm the first two weeks of February, and most of our snow had melted—a false promise, of course. Three inches of fresh, wet snow had fallen overnight and now covered the muddy, debris-littered landscape that surfaces with the first melt every year. Even though it was mid-February, Ollie Lundeen who works part-time at the cemetery, had managed to get the grave open with his new backhoe. When we passed through the two cinder block pillars that guard the entrance to the North Haven Cemetery, he was standing next to the still-shiny machine about thirty yards up the rise. He was leaning proudly on the fender as we gathered around the hole he had just gauged in the even white sea of snow.

In recent years, cemeteries have come to believe that it is indiscreet for anyone attending an interment to be disturbed by the sight of raw earth. Doubtless they have been so persuaded by salesmen who sell the green indoor-outdoor carpeting used to cover that offending pile of dirt next to the grave and to surround the hole itself like surgical drapes cover an abdomen during an operation. But being green, when set atop the morning's three inches of fresh snow, it fooled no one. In time the cemetery carpet salesmen will doubtless come to recognize a potential market for white cemetery carpet in northerly places. But for Anna-Lena, any carpet on the pile of dirt would have doubtless been yet another instance of "making a fuss."

Lamont, the oldest of the boys, who was back from the Cities for the service, had asked me if I would help out as a pallbearer. They were short on pallbearers, he said. Short of people under eighty would have been more precise. I have filled in as a guest pallbearer more than once. He recruited an undertaker as well, and the six of us, the three grandsons, a son, a mortician from New Ulm, and the minister, lined up in two rows of three, facing each other at the back of the hearse. We carried the casket, which surely weighed twice its contents, up the slight hill, watching our footing in the wet snow, and placed it on the sawhorses, green sawhorses, at the head of the grave. I then moved to the downhill side of the hole and, when the circle of mourners was closed, began to read the brief interment service out of the old *Book of Common Worship*, replete with all the "thee's" and "thou's" and "wouldst's" and "shouldst's." Yet another fuss of course, but this was the faux-Elizabethan English that Anna-Lena's generation had learned to speak in their discourse with God.

I read the Twenty-third Psalm and noted that the only hint of "green pastures" was the carpet surrounding the grave. I read Newman's timeless prayer to close: "O Lord, support us all the day long, until the shadows lengthen and the evening comes, and the busy world is hushed and the fever of life is over and our work is done. Then in Thy mercy, grant us a safe lodging and a holy rest and peace at last." The most perfect sentence in the English language, some critic had once judged it, though actually it is two. I closed my prayer book and handed it to Ardis Wilcox to hold. Her husband had just given me a too-obvious directive nod with his head. Speech seemed out of place at the moment, but Jimmy's message was clear: "You and I are going to take the other end of the casket, and then the six of us are going to lift it off the sawhorses and lay it on the two-by-sixes over the grave." None of this had been rehearsed, just some last-minute strategy whispered by the funeral director as we stood at the hearse door.

I put on my gloves, looked back at Jimmy, tilted my head uphill, and raised my eyebrows inquiringly to confirm his message. He replied with another, even more dramatic nod, and we turned in sync to move decorously around the grave to the foot end of the casket. That uphill side of the grave offered but a narrow passage between the carpet-covered pile of earth and the black hole. I moved carefully but knew I would be safe if I kept my feet on the carpet. I remember thinking this to myself as I stepped in front of Larry to the foot of the grave, and then made a longish stride that I judged would land me on green carpet on the other side. I stepped on the edge of the carpet, but where I stepped green carpet did not cover firm earth. I stepped where green carpet covered nothing but the edge of open grave dug generously wide by Ollie's new backhoe. I emitted what Larry later described as "a long whoa" as I slipped into Anna-Lena's grave. I didn't fall all the way, thank God, just one leg of me. The other stayed on green carpet, and as I went down I caught myself on one of the two-by-sixes stretched over the hole.

In the proverbial twinkling of an eye, I was splayed and suspended, half in this world, half in the next, one foot literally in the grave. The entire graveside congregation gasped in a unison as precise any perfect "amen" at the end of a hymn. Larry and Lamont fished me out. When it was clear that nothing was broken, a dozen hands covered a dozen mouths suddenly trespassing into unseemly mirth. At first it appeared that the only damage done was a muddy shoe and wounded pride.

I rode back to the church in the backseat of Jimmy's car, watching the mud on my loafers dry from black to reddish-brown. My back was beginning to hurt. I had pulled something, and no position achievable in the rear seat of a '93 Monte Carlo relieved the increasingly sharp jabs of pain. Ardis had chuckled when she pulled the front seat-back forward so I could climb in the back. She looked down at my shoe and, proud of her wit, had said, "Feet of clay, isn't that what they say, Reverend?" Twenty years ago, I thought, even ten years ago, this would never have happened. My stride would have been longer; I would have seen that the carpet extended over the hole itself. My bifocals were to blame. I had them on for reading my prayer book and strong bifocals make things down by your feet look fuzzy and out of place. "Feet of clay" was not what I was thinking. The cliché that I could not expel from my mind was "one foot in the grave."

This fourteenth of February was the twentieth Valentine's Day that Annie and I would celebrate together. We had decided to attend to the day more closely than we had in recent years, and I had made reservations at the River's Edge in Mankato the day before. I learned that Annie had bought a new dress for the occasion when she saw me walk into the kitchen in the cautious gait of those who suffer lower back pain. I was carrying my shoes, one still caked with mud.

"What happened to you?" she asked.

"I fell in Anna-Lena's grave," I answered, no inflection to my voice.

She covered her mouth to hide her smile just like everyone at the cemetery had. "Well, we *are* going to dinner," she said. "I bought a new dress. This is Valentine's Day number twenty, and I want to go to Mankato."

The River's Edge Supper Club does not offer what the larger world would judge a gourmet dining experience. Built in the sixties, it is a single story frame building ensconced in dented white aluminum siding, its low roof crowned with a diadem of heating and air-conditioning units. It sits on the edge of a bluff just south of Highway 14 west of Mankato. The Minnesota River is just visible, but only in the winter through leafless trees and a parade of power lines. In this part of the world "supper club" was once the term that clued the cognoscenti to a public secret. Not only was a "supper club" a restaurant that was open at night, unlike "cafés" "diners," "coffee shops," and "luncheonettes," but supper clubs either had a liquor license, or if the county was dry, let you brown-bag it. The wine list at the River's Edge is not long: "red, white, or blush." The specialty of the house is prime rib. In fact, there is a large color painting of a slab of rare prime rib on the sign out front.

There are finer restaurants in Mankato, but this one is on our edge of town, and we wanted to get home for the kids before it got too late and the food is, as advertised, "fine." But as we pulled into the parking lot and dodged the growing crop of midwinter potholes that had blossomed in the lot, I asked myself if, at this stage of my life, I couldn't have done better. Annie was undaunted by either the potholes in the parking lot or the painting of the prime rib on the sign out front. Ever since she had come downstairs and slipped on her coat, I had seen that her eye held a restrained glimmer. I know my wife well enough to know when she is keeping a secret.

Our easy banter on the drive over had masked some anticipation on her part. She was obviously waiting for something. It could hardly be the River's Edge, I thought to myself. I hung up our coats on the wall hooks near the front door and walked behind her to our table by a big picture window overlooking the falling darkness. I was beginning to worry that she had violated our Valentine's Day covenant and bought me a gift. We had agreed on cards only and had exchanged them with the kids before leaving. But she had no package hidden on her person. Indeed, my wife was wearing a dress that would not permit the secreting of any package, even the tiniest, on her person. It was a stunning dress, a shimmering burgundy: modest by New York City standards, deserving of comment in Mankato, and nothing she could ever wear in North Haven, even if she were not the minister's wife. There was simply no imaginable North Haven occasion at which such a dress would have been remotely appropriate. It was not a strapless dress, however. Indeed, the straps that lay over her shoulders were fairly wide. My wife, less than accustomed to such evening wear, was fussing with them repeatedly, making sure they were just where they were supposed to be.

We waited to order. I was nursing a glass of wine—"the red"; Annie was sipping a Diet Sprite. Across the table from me sat a woman far lovelier than this old preacher with one foot in the grave deserved. My back was still aching, but I was as comfortable as I had been for some hours in one of the River's Edge avocado-green vinyl chairs. I thought to myself, "Here sits a woman far more indulgent, far more patient with me and the church than this tired supper club in western Minnesota deserves." While I was burying Anna-Lena that afternoon, it had struck me that I was now pressing beyond precise middle age, even by her lofty standard of ninety-four years. Everyone would classify forty-seven as "middle age," but how many ninety-four-year-olds do you know? I shifted in my chair and a stab of pain ran up my aching back. My brooding mood was not shared by my wife, who was looking ever more like a schoolgirl out for the night in a place she wasn't supposed to be. She had something up her sleeve, but she had no sleeves.

Finally she reached across the table and lay her hand on mine and held my eye in a way that asked for silence. With her other hand she moved the strap of her dress slightly, just to the edge of her shoulder. She looked down and I followed her gaze.

"What's that?" I asked, staring at what looked to my far-sighted eyes like a brown-black splotch about an inch across and six inches below her shoulder.

"It's not permanent," she answered.

"But what is it," I pressed. "I left my glasses in the

car, Annie, I can't see what it is. Are you okay, Honey?"

I was leaning forward across the table. I pushed the red carnation in the carnival glass vase to the side so I could get a closer look. I squinted like an old man in the dim light in the restaurant. My presbyopia (ironic name for the far-sightedness that comes to most of us with age) kept the mark that my wife had kept hidden under her dress hidden from my eyes.

Just then our waitress was back for our order. She was about nineteen and had introduced herself saying, "Hi, I'm Jessica, I'll be your server tonight." She watched the scene with incredulity for a few seconds, and then took off her fashionable wire-rimmed glasses and handed them to me. "Here, try these sir." They were too small for me to get the bows over my ears, so I held them like a pince-nez, moving them back and forth to focus on the spot on my wife's shoulder, still squinting. Annie was giggling. It was a tattoo, a tiny heart pierced by an arrow. Perched along the shaft of the arrow were four neat block letters spelling "D-A-V-E."

"It'll wash off, it's just temporary," she said. "I bought it at Mall of America last summer. I wrote in your name with eyeliner. Happy Valentine's Day, Honey."

The irony of it all collapsed on me as I collapsed back in my Naugahyde chair. When my wife was younger, she would have never done such a thing. But she has shed most of her erstwhile primness with the years. She had come to that ironic intersection in life where she would and still could wear a fetching burgundy dress and a temporary tattoo, yet her aging husband was too presbyopic to see either of them clearly.

We drove home saying little, occasionally holding hands across the center console of the Taurus. One of the blessings of twenty years of marriage is that silence in each other's presence comes to be comfortable. My back hurt and so did my pride. I had had to ask the waitress to lend me her glasses again so that I could read the menu. A few miles out of town, the epistle text for the Sunday coming started to run through my mind. I still had no idea what I would say about it come Sunday. It was Paul at his most labyrinthine, his rambling meditation in Romans 4 on the story of Abraham and Sarah. That patriarch and matriarch are even more ancient than my wife and I and had spent a lifetime hoping against hope for the child they have been promised. In the original account of the incident in Genesis, Sarah had laughed when visiting angels had stopped in to promise a child, though Paul discreetly omits that detail when he retells the tale. Like my wife, Sarah must have had the richer sense of humor in that family too. "Abraham," Paul noted for his readers' moral benefit, "did not weaken in faith when he considered his own body, which was already as good as dead, for he was about one hundred years old." I wondered if Abraham had a bad back when he was a hundred.

Dark miles of Highway 14 rolled by. We passed through one little town after another, all pretty much closed down at 9:00 p.m.: Nicollet, then Courtland and New Ulm, the last of which still did bear some signs of life into the evening. We passed through Essig and last of all Sleepy Eye. How was it again that the place came to have such a comic name? Days roll by in the same way, like a string of little towns. You pass through them and see what there is to see. I like to think that even the most ordinary of them has its attractions. They say that Darwin up on U.S. 12 just west of Minneapolis has the world's largest ball of twine. You leave each of them behind, the lights of the last gas station finally disappearing in your rearview mirror, and remember that there is always another just down the road. Always one more little town, and then you're home.

We got back about 9:30. The kids were still up, of course. A warmish breeze—it must have been at least forty degrees—was melting what remained of last night's wet snow. We sat on the front stoop before going in the house. That stoop, too, was my wife's idea. We opened our coats in the near-warmth and listened to the breeze and the bursts of canned laughter from the television sit-com the kids were watching in the living room. I looked at my shoe, the one that had descended into the grave earlier in the day. It had cleaned up well enough with a couple of paper towels, but I had not had time to polish it.

Just to the left of my shoe, barely visible in the melting snow, was an early crocus, a snowdrop, living white against the frozen white of the snow, pushing its head hopefully above the crystals. It was too early and almost imperceptible. I reached for it as Annie spoke. She had been gazing across the street and had not seen me looking at the flower.

She said, "David, I didn't want to make a scene in the restaurant." I sat up straight; I forgot the snowdrop and my sore back. My wife never calls me David. "I know how you can get," she continued. "I've got some news, I mean news. David, I'm not sure, but I think I'm pregnant."

— 8 —

March 21, Ash Wednesday

An Answer to Prayer

O my God, I cry by day, but thou dost not answer. . .

—Psalm 22:2

The Brook View Adult Care Facility is this side of Sleepy Eye and faces Highway 14 like a long, single-story motel, except there are no outside doors to the rooms. The single front door opens into a small lobby furnished with several clusters of box-like modern chairs upholstered in burgundy Herculon. On the coffee table at the center of each cluster lie neatly fanned piles of magazines, *Good Housekeeping*, *Sports Afield*, and *Modern Maturity.* The receptionist faces the front door just beyond the lobby. She reigns ensconced in a rectangular cubicle, the ledges of which are just high enough for her to see over from her chair. To her left and to her right are two long hallways. Behind her is the dining area, one corner of which doubles as the "Arts and Crafts Area," where two folding tables topped in faux wood sit deserted and surrounded by empty fiberglass chairs. In the other corner of the open room, under a sign that reads "Friendship Center," four old ladies play a quiet hand of whist. There is indeed a brook, but it is not easily viewed, save from several choice end-rooms on the back side of the building.

From her vantage point, the smiley overweight receptionist, whose badge announces her to be "Krista," can see not only the front entrance, but all the way down both halls as well as the entire dining area behind her. The suspended sign over Krista's head reads "Reception." She is indeed charged with receiving visitors like me, which she did with a smile and a Minnesota "hi"—a long, flat diphthong rising and ascending a note and a half as she dragged it out. But Krista had also been stationed where she could keep an eye out for any Brook View residents who might be prone to wander. It would be no small matter to bust out of Brook View, but as would become apparent in a few months, it could be done.

"Mrs. MacDowell is in 38," said Krista without consulting the computer screen in front of her. She pointed with her pencil down the long hall to her right, "It's the seventh door on your left, Reverend, just before the nurse's station."

They say that one of the few physical advantages of aging is that you catch fewer colds. By the time you're ninety, you've encountered most every one of them and your body is an Alexandrian library of antibodies. But just after Christmas Minnie MacDowell's immune system had encountered a virus that was not in her private collection. What had first been a stubborn midwinter cold soon descended into bronchitis. By the last week of January, she was in the Lutheran Hospital with pneumonia. When the worst of it had cleared up a week later, she was still too sick for Angus to look after at home. At Dr. Wilson's polite but unyielding insistence, Minnie had been discharged from the hospital directly to Brook View.

"Just till she gets her strength back," he had said to both of them as Angus turned to leave Minnie's hospital room to go get the car.

Minnie had added, "Won't be more than a few weeks, Angus. Just go fetch the car, and remember to warm it up good."

But a few weeks had now grown into two months. Minnie was indeed a little stronger, but Parkinson's had made a battle with a truculent virus into trench warfare. And though pneumonia may retreat, Parkinson's does not. For a decade and a half, hers had marched upon her with a blessed lethargy, but now allied with great age and sudden frailty, the disease advanced ruthlessly. I found her in Room 38 sitting in a wheelchair on the other side of the bed with her back to the door. She was looking out the large single window at Highway 14. Several cars passed a John Deere tractor slowly pulling a disc harrow east.

"Knock, knock," I said. "Are you receiving?" I used

that word playfully, but I also knew that Minnie relished all the little accouterments of the old formality.

She turned her head slowly to my voice, offered a bare smile, every bit as demonstrative as the disease permitted, and said, "David."

At some intersection in these last weeks, Minnie had ceased calling me "Pastor" and had taken to using my Christian name. It was a change of manner that ran counter to the inertia of centuries of Protestant decorum. After hearing her call me nothing but "Pastor" for ten years, every time I hear my first name on her lips, it rings like a daring intimacy. Again it struck me that intimacy so often follows close on the heels of vulnerability. Minnie appeared disarmingly vulnerable. She was dressed in a powder blue housecoat, her fleece-lined leather slippers perched on the footrests of the wheel chair. An aide had run a brush through her hair, but it was months since it had been permed into the tight curls she favored.

She began there, of course, apologizing for her hair. "A girl comes in on Fridays to do hair, but she's not Barbara. I'm going to wait till I get home, so Barbara can do it."

I sat on the edge of the tightly made bed and said, "I'm sure she'd drive out here and do your hair, Minnie."

She had doubtless already considered this, and she dismissed the suggestion quickly, saying, "It would probably hurt the feelings of the girl they got here. Anyway, I'll be home soon."

"How you doing, Minnie? You feeling stronger?"

"They say the pneumonia is better. But it takes its toll on you when you're not so young. The doctors are doing everything, too much if you ask me, but they can't fix Parkinson's."

We talked about health, the food at Brook View, Angus, and, of course, James. "Angus is no good at this," Minnie observed. This was a judgment I assumed covered illness, care giving, perhaps even the prospect of being a widower. "Won't talk about it, of course. When I'm home he fusses around like an old lady. Asks me every ten minutes if I'm better yet and what can he get for me."

"James is keeping him company, isn't he? I mean after school and for dinner."

"Oh, sure. Angus had him up here to visit the day before yesterday. The kid was tearing up and down the hall, seeing how far he could slide in his stocking feet on the wax. Knocked into a dinner cart and spilled cranberry juice all over the place."

Along with Minnie's use of my first name had come an even more uncharacteristic attitude of indulgence, even appreciation, for James Corey's unbounded energy and penchant for spilling liquid things, breaking delicate things, and knocking over anything within a ten-foot radius of his constantly kinetic little body.

She was surely smiling at the thought of it. But Minnie's smiles are now barely to be seen, veiled as they are by the Parkinson's. She knew I understood this and went on about the child that had brought such unruly life into theirs these two years.

"When the two of them left, James sneaked back in to talk to me while Angus was in the bathroom down the hall. He comes up to me and cups his hand around my good ear and whispers, very serious, 'Minnie, I said a prayer for you to get better.' "

She raised a trembling hand to her mouth to demonstrate James's whisper. "Then he says to me, 'You tell God that you want to get better from the disease, and he'll make you better. Mrs. Gottliebsen says that God answers all our prayers. No lie, Minnie, no lie. She's a Sunday school teacher. She knows.' Such trust in that little rascal's heart," Minnie added. She then looked back at Highway 14 and was silent for a moment. "David, the truth is, I hardly know what to pray for anymore. Ten, twelve years ago, when they first said the word, I prayed to be healed. For years, I prayed that God would just take it away."

Her words came in a steady monotone beat, like a soft drum, without emotional affect, their Parkinson's flatness belying the power underneath them. "I prayed, and nothing changed. Oh, it came on slow, maybe God gave me that. But slow was not what I prayed for. Finally I stopped praying to be cured. I stopped the day that I remembered that wolf."

Intrigued as I was at her mention of a wolf, I saw that she was already looking exhausted and was hesitant to invite more words. "Are you getting tired, Minnie?" I asked. It was hard to tell what tired might look like on her.

"Yes, a little, but David, I want to tell you about it. It's eighty years ago now and I've never told a soul, not even Angus."

I had been preparing to invite her to pray, the routine punctuation that ends most such visits. But instead I crossed my legs, pulling my ankle up on my knee, looking ready to stay. Minnie clearly had more on her mind than pastoral prayers.

"I was thirteen years old. It was 1918, March of 1918, a Tuesday. The twelfth it was. I can tell you the date exactly. I was in the eighth grade. My family had a farm in Otter Tail County, Sverdrup Township. All four of my grandparents had homesteaded in the same part of the county. My parents lived their lives there until they retired. They sold the farm and moved into Fergus Falls. Winters run hard up there, you know, much colder than down here. Oh, there were some real bad years back then. Sometimes we were hungry, the whole county was hungry."

She was clearly exhausted but finding power in memory and in the telling of it. "On the twelfth of March, 1918, a prairie wolf followed me home from school. I was walking the right-hand rut of a two-rut road, alongside our cornfield, just stubble in March, of course. I remember the snow was lying only in the furrows, blown in there by the wind. It was like black and white stripes. I saw him in the woods on the other side of the field. Every once and again, he would move out of the woods, and I would see him moving along with me; he was watching me. He kept up with me for maybe half an hour. He was all bone, he was. Sometimes he would stop and lower his head and just look at me. I was scared, but I was afraid to run, like running would let him know I was alive. So I just walked real steady and watched him without turning to look. And David, I prayed. I prayed like I never prayed in my life."

"And here you are," I said, too glib and eager for answered prayer.

"Yes, here I am, eighty-four years later. It was 1918. The Spanish Influenza. I ran the last hundred yards and burst through the door glad to be alive. My parents and brother looked up at me from the kitchen table. Their eyes were red, I remember how their eyes were red. I'll never forget it, the three of them sitting there, looking at me. My father got up and came to me. I can still see him. He took me by both shoulders and looked down at me and told me that Gert had just died, not ten minutes ago. They had just come downstairs from our room. Then he held me tight, so tight it almost hurt. I remember that especially, how tight he held me. And then he sobbed. Not for the whole of your life do you forget it when you see your parents weep. That was the only time I ever saw him cry. I don't know that my mother ever did. Gertrude was my older sister. She was fourteen. I never even told them about the wolf. Never told anybody till now."

I said nothing. I knew Minnie had more to say and needed no coaxing.

"It was like God had answered my prayers when the

wolf was following me home. So the wolf let me go, but he came for Gertrude. That's what I thought. For years, I thought it must have been my fault. It was like my prayers had caused it. I know other families had it worse in the influenza, but I adored her, David. Why didn't God answer all those prayers for Gert?"

Minnie turned away from me and watched the occasional sparse traffic on the highway. No tears now; neither of us spoke. The silence was eloquent enough. Compassion is sometimes extended as much in the words you don't say as it is in those you do.

"I stopped praying that Parkinson's would leave me alone because I remembered the wolf, the wolf and Gertrude and the Spanish Influenza. I was afraid of what my prayers might do. I didn't pray for two, three years. I ached to, but the old words wouldn't come. And then finally, after all these years, I finally decided that it wasn't my fault. I decided it was never Gertrude instead of me. I prayed again, but I said bigger prayers. I just tell Him what I think and how I feel. I don't much tell Him what to do. I just tell Him I'm afraid, afraid for me and afraid for the boys and afraid for that old fool of a husband. I suppose He knows it all already, but words make it solid. I always whispered them at night when I was awake, listening to Angus snoring."

I watched the Highway 14 traffic with her, the old lady in her wheelchair, I on her bed, both of us looking out the window as the afternoon faded into dusk. I had no quick words in the face of her transparency, but knew only candor would do. "I do think God answers prayer," I answered. "But I'm not sure anymore just what it means. I've watched too many people pray their hearts out and get nothing that looked like an answer. And then I've watched folks pray for miracles and get them. I don't know."

"Well, Pastor, don't worry. This old lady's prayers have been answered." Minnie MacDowell suddenly switched to the formalities of Protestant address to preach her sermon. "Not the answers I wanted, though. God didn't take away the Parkinson's, but he did take away the fear."

Some answer to prayer, I thought.

Minnie asked if she could pray with me. She turned her wheelchair away from the window and with some difficulty wheeled it a foot toward me. She reached for my hands and as she held them, our four hands trembled together. She spoke a few words, flat and rambling, about peace and trust. Then she asked God to bless me and my family, and Angus and their boys, and James. Inarticulate as it may have been, that prayer was nothing less than belief answering unbelief.

I drove west on the very Highway 14 Minnie and I had watched together. I dared not pray, but wondered how God would answer my prayers of late. I had been praying for my church. The annual fall stewardship financial campaign for the next year's budget had gone poorly. Rather, it had gone well. Everyone said it was informative and challenging, and many people had increased their pledges but there were seven fewer of them. This last year saw several deaths and three more families move out of town. This sweet place that has so tenaciously held our hearts is not holding on to its sons and daughters. The Lyric Odeon closed this winter. The Piggly Wiggly is going to close the end of the month.

Last fall I had a call from the Methodist district superintendent to explore the prospect of a church union between North Haven Methodists and the Presbyterians, or perhaps, he hinted, "some sort of a pastor-sharing arraignment." The hard truth, emerging slowly upon all of us, is that Second Presbyterian can no more afford a full-time minister than can Aldersgate Methodist. For years I suppose that I had prayed for something like ecclesiastical prosperity so that our life could continue to be as it has been.

That prayer had not been answered, at least not with the answer it leaned into. Answers that lean the other way have come at last, hardly what I had ever prayed for. First came a phone call from the Pastor Nominating Committee of Westminster Presbyterian Church, Elm Forest, Michigan. They were looking for a new minister. Would I read their Church Information Form and consider discussing the matter?

Elm Forest, I learned by reading entirely between the lines of the boosterish document that arrived four days later with the tell-tale return address omitted, is a blue-collar downriver suburb of Detroit, built quick and cheap in the space of ten years in the late fifties and early sixties. Surely no elms were left, probably no forest at all. But the chair of the committee was patient and frankly honest on the phone. He was seasoned well beyond the Chamber of Commerce salesmanship of the

Church Information Form I had just read. He described a suburb bordered by four others with sound-alike names, all filled with waves of tract houses. He talked about the problems they faced: stressed-out families, drugs and alcohol, a school system past its prime. Then he talked with obvious affection about a stubbornly faithful church of four hundred members who cared about each other and the place they lived. He said the building was built in 1963 and might best be described as "practical." It had a brand-new roof though—almost paid for—and no steeple.

That phone call had led to a visit to North Haven a few weeks later from Walt Ungerer, the nominating committee chairman, and two other committee members, Tracie, who taught the fifth and sixth grade Sunday school class, and Irma, the apparent committee matriarch and, she noted, "twice past-moderator of the Women's Association." Their visit had led to an invitation to come to Elm Forest the week after Easter to meet the entire committee of six and preach for them in a neutral pulpit. This was hardly the answer to prayer I had in mind.

Yet another unanticipated answer arrived with the New Year in the guise of Melinda Ackermann, the new United Methodist pastor, half-time, underemployed, and underpaid by her dwindling flock at Aldersgate Methodist. She was second-career, forty-ish, divorced, gregarious, bright, and easy to like. She was from Redwood Falls and would take to North Haven. And North Haven, perhaps even the Presbyterians, would surely take to her. Another answer to prayer perhaps, but again, hardly the one I had imagined. So, yes, Minnie, God does answer prayer. But you're right, time and again it invites answers you never imagined. It is indeed a good idea to pray big.

— 9 —

April 7, Easter Sunday

Ten-Point Sermon

O death, where is thy victory?
O death, where is thy sting?
—1 Corinthians 15:55

Another white Easter, but just barely. Holy Week had blown up from the south, warm and wet, noisy and full of promises. Friday had turned still and bitter cold and froze the thousand puddles of Thursday into a thousand mirrors. Saturday it snowed ever so gently into the late evening, a bare inch perhaps, just enough to bless the hard black mud of spring delayed again.

I wanted to be early at church, so I was up well before sunrise. I brewed coffee and set off on the four-block walk with a Dunkin' Donuts travel mug in one hand and an English muffin dripping raspberry jam in the other. I wanted a couple hours with my sermon, a careful and, I feared, labored exposition of resurrection that lay flat on its back on the desk in my study. It was in need of something more than polishing. As every honest preacher knows, Easter is notoriously daunting to preach. There are no mortal words sleek enough to speak lightning. As often as not come Easter morning, the music and lilies have to carry the day.

I fretted as to how the old story would be told fresh after the sun rose in this particular place on this particular Easter, the billionth telling in the billionth place. Words could hold Him no more than tombs. I remembered an image that still hung fast in my mind from seminary. It was offered by a young lecturer in New Testament quoting Barth, if I recall rightly. Reading the Bible, he had said, is like sitting at your desk looking out the study window and watching people who are very excited about something. They are running and jumping about, urgently pointing upward. You can see their enthusiasm and you can hear their cries, but sitting where you sit, you cannot see what they see.

The wet snow crunched under my boots. It was everywhere untrodden, virgin. This preacher, like Mary Magdalene, was the first one up. Light was just cracking the horizon, deep dawn an inch before sunrise. Lifting my coffee cup to my lips, I looked down at the snow in front of me and saw tracks. Perfection had been disturbed by light feet, wandering, paying no heed to where the sidewalk might lie under the snow. They led away toward the church, going on before me. Sometime in the night, perhaps just a moment ago, another deer had wandered into town. This was no longer an unusual occurrence. By the look of the prints, it was a good-sized animal, probably a buck. I was not the first one up on Easter morning after all.

I followed the tracks for a while—they were leading me where I was going anyway—until they turned aside into Bud Jennerson's driveway. I could see them trail off behind his new detached double garage toward the sunny spot where Bud plants tomatoes and string beans every spring. I walked on past his house and the next, remembering the last time I had come upon a deer.

As I mused, the buck stepped out in front of me from behind an overgrown yew at the far corner of the next house. He had circled around in back of the Gunderson's, either to meet me or to elude me. I gasped and dropped my half-full coffee mug, which landed quietly on the snow-covered grass next to the sidewalk. For two, maybe three seconds, an eternity to be sure, he stood in my path and looked at me. His brown-black eyes held mine defiantly. As I stared at him, I swear I saw my reflection in his unblinking eye, a startled-still Mary Magdalene in a parka with fake-fur around the hood holding a red-smeared English muffin in his hand. I looked between and above the eyes, and there in the hair that covered the hard cartilage at the base of his antlers was a scar. It was an ugly bald crater less than an inch across. No blood now, but it was just where it would be.

He snorted as he raised his head and turned away, quite casually. Then he didn't so much as bolt as he leaped three times with early morning grace, turned to me again, and walked off delicately so as to say, "I do not fear you." I stood stock still as I watched him retreat, away from town now, north. I bent over to retrieve the empty Dunkin' Donuts mug at my feet. Coffee stained the snow around it like old dried blood.

The six typescript pages of resurrection still lay flat on my desk when I arrived at my study. I looked down at them, but all I could see was the look in his eyes, the first time and again this morning. So when I climbed into the pulpit three hours later, I began not where I had planned, but where I had been led. "Something happened early this morning on the way to church. Probably a coincidence. Even if that's all it is, coincidences may be God's way of maintaining anonymity. I'm not sure what it means, if it means anything at all, but it begs telling. And it may be a door into Easter."

Then I read some disconnected verses from Paul's resurrection chapter in 1 Corinthians, older words than any of the four Gospels. These were a reprise to the morning's Gospel reading, noted in the bulletin, which had already been read. Chapter 15 of that first letter to Corinth is a hymnic montage, poetry scattered and less than sequential in its logic, but glorious words, nearly sleek enough to speak lightning: "There is one glory of the sun, and another glory of the moon, and another glory of the stars . . . so it is with their resurrection. . . . Lo, I tell you a mystery. We shall not all sleep, but we shall all be changed in the twinkling of an eye. . . . Death is swallowed up in victory. O death, where is thy victory? O death, where is thy sting?"

So I wound my way into the Easter mystery with the story of the morning walk to church and the buck that moved out from behind the Gunderson's yew and was so audacious as to hold my gaze for an eternal moment before he leapt up high and turned to me again. As best as words allowed, I described his defiant eyes, and then I noted the scar at the base of his rack. "It was a ten-point rack," I said. "I didn't count this morning. I didn't need to. I had counted them before."

Illustrating resurrection with a deer hunting tale is less irreverent than I would have once imagined. Hunting is one of life's givens in this place, an annual rhythm that serves as one of the marks of fall's advent, along with the first hard frost and the smell of burning leaves. Hunting is not in the least controversial. My high-school senior daughter is the only antihunting advocate in town. She even converted to vegetarianism last year, which gave her opinions on hunting an edge of credibility. Willful as she is, she is savvy enough to preach her sermon on hunting only to me and her mother, a sermon that is invariably and generously peppered with the word, "Neanderthal."

She had preached it that evening last November when I accepted the Wilcox brothers' invitation to do some deer hunting the next Saturday. She had overheard my end of the phone call and protested my uncharacteristic decision to go out for the day. Then she pronounced hunting to be brutal and, well, "Neanderthal." I brought it to her attention that she was wearing leather shoes. She looked down at them, hesitated, and said, "I bet the cow died of old age." I said, "I doubt it."

White-tailed deer abound throughout the state of Minnesota, to the point of being both nuisance and traffic hazard. The animals wander into town, nibbling at gardens and landscape shrubbery. I was not raised in a hunting world, and when we first moved here I met it with something between disinterest and distaste. Even though logic can judge sport no crueler than abattoir, I stood quietly back from it. But when you stay in one place for some time, you fall an inch a day into its ways. Its words and its unspoken assumptions overtake you. And so it was with me and hunting. Hunting and fishing were also, I came to understand, the door into something like male camaraderie. I knew that men sometimes allowed a shadow of intimacy with other men over beer, perhaps even coffee. But it was hunting and fishing that created a distinct male space where words that would otherwise be unspoken might comfortably be uttered. My wife told me I needed that, and I knew she was right.

So when Jimmy phoned, I said yes, also feeling flattered at being included in a day of hunting that was planned as something of a Wilcox boys' reunion. He offered to lend me his old 94 Winchester 30-30. He said he was feeling tired all the time, but insisted on going along and sitting the day out in Lamont's Explorer.

"Some big buck probably come along and give me a heart attack," he muttered. "Either that or I'd keel over draggin' him out of the woods."

I told the congregation none of this on Easter morning. It was only preface, and most of them knew it anyway. They knew that the minister went hunting with the Wilcox boys last fall. They also knew that he had lost Jimmy's Winchester out in the woods north of town, the very gun his father had given him for his eighteenth birthday. But just how I came to lose it in the woods they did not know Lamont and Larry, who both saw it happen, and Jimmy whom they told when it was fresh and savory, had collectively offered to keep it under their hats. They judged the tale not only bizarre, but also vaguely embarrassing to me.

> "You know that the Wilcox boys and I went deer hunting last fall," I went on. "Right here in the county. Just for the day. We went out just before dawn the Saturday after opening day. We had our coffee by the truck. Lamont and I went off to the east over a cornfield toward some low-lying sumac and popple next to a stand of maples just beyond the old Goerke farm."

I did not mention that as we waited for the sun, Jimmy had held the Thermos cap of coffee cradled in his hands and had talked about his son, Jason. It was a parent's lament, no more or no less. He was looking for no counsel, only shoulders to share the burden.

I told a congregation growing intrigued with an unlikely Easter sermon,

> "Larry was circling around to the side of the small woods. Likely place for deer this time of the year. He said that if he didn't get a shot himself, he would drive any animals that might be back in there out for the two of us."

As I told the tale I did not mention that, though I had never before hunted game bigger than snipe, I was in fact a rather good shot. Thirty-some years ago my father, grasping for some father and son activity I would deign to share with him, had hit upon skeet shooting. Boys liked guns, he figured, so together we shot skeet—clay pigeons—those fast-flying discs flung into our sights by a mechanical arm at the Peeksborough Skeet Range. We did this many a Saturday through the silent and moody passages of my adolescence. We spoke little, but came nearer in the silence between shots. My father said I was a natural.

I continued:

"Well, Larry drove a big buck out of the wood. Lamont and I were still crossing the corn stubble. The deer pushed his way through the underbrush to the edge of the sumac and stood there, not fifty yards from us. Lamont said to me, 'David, he's yours.' I aimed between the eyes, a clear shot and a clean kill. He bowed to me ever so slightly as I pulled the trigger. He dropped right there. Lamont and I ran across the corn stubble. He lifted the animal's head by the rack and counted the points on his antlers. 'Ten-point buck, Pastor. Not bad, not bad at all. And lookie here, you almost hit him between the eyes. Just a little high. You must be a natural!' Larry arrived a moment later, with his camera, of course." (At this a wave of knowing laughter rolled through the pews.) "Larry said a photo was a must and that there was only one way to do it. He told me to kneel down and hold up the buck's head by his rack. Then he told Lamont to lay my rifle, actually Jimmy Wilcox's 94 Winchester 30-30, horizontally across the antlers.

"I knelt beside the animal, warm and still. His head was heavier than I had imagined. It was awkward to lift and hold still. Lamont laid the rifle across the rack and moved back beside his brother who was focusing and deciding whether or not to use the flash. He held up his hand, took a step back, and said, 'Hold it right there.' The flash went off . . . and with a start, the buck shook his antlers free of my hands. He struggled powerfully to his feet as I fell back on my rear. He snorted and jerked his head back. Then he turned and leapt three times toward the tangle of sumac. But before he went back into the woods beyond, he turned and looked at me. His dark, glass-like eyes held nothing so much as defiance. His antlers held nothing but Jimmy's Winchester 30-30. He went into the woods carrying the very instrument of his death high and proud."

It was defiance I preached, for Easter is just that. This one bold creature of God had mocked death once and mocked me twice. Resurrection, I preached, is the forever mocking of the last enemy. Until this morning, I had always imagined the Risen Christ with compassion in his eyes; now I imagine raw defiance.

I can't prove a thing, of course. But I have good

reason to trust those who are leaping about and pointing outside my window, among them Paul and Mary Magdalene (such an unlikely pair), jabbing their fingers at something I cannot see from where I sit. But maybe I do see something of what they see, at least the down-to-earth shadows of some higher movement. I see it in all things lovelier than they need to be, in people kinder than you would expect, in unanticipated recoveries, in entirely gratuitous graces, in truth found out of place.

I can't prove a thing, of course. I can only trust God to be God. And if God be God, this One who pulled five billion galaxies out of compacted matter, hurled planets into their places, and then imagined the lady slipper, can certainly defy death in the twinkling of an eye. That is where you see such death-defying defiance—in the eyes.

— 10 —

May 13

The Wolf Up North

Then I saw a new heaven and a new earth, for the first heaven and the first earth had passed away. . . . And he who sat on the throne said, "Behold, I make all things new."

—Revelation 21:1, 5

Stillwater is an old and once-gracious river town that grew tired in the years after the great lumber boom. It lies the other side of the St. Paul, set in the hills that tumble down to the banks of the St. Croix and rise on the other side as Wisconsin. In recent years better highways have connected the town to the Twin Cities, and it has slowly become what its founders never imagined: a suburb, albeit a suburb with an old soul. But to many in Minnesota, the name Stillwater does not evoke so much the river or the lumber trade, much less suburbia; Stillwater means the prison. Like Leavenworth or Ossining ("Sing Sing"), in this corner of the world Stillwater is a sideways name for incarceration. "Kid's gonna end up in Stillwater," is the dour prophecy long uttered over budding juvenile delinquents all across the state.

These words had never been spoken about Jason Wilcox, whom I was driving to visit in Stillwater on a grim May morning. People had said, "That kid's gonna end up in Willmar," which was, if anything, an even crueler prognostication. Willmar, a hundred miles to the north of North Haven, was for decades the home of one of those vast state mental institutions that enlightened reformers built a century ago, a leafy campus of gloomy red brick buildings that have now emptied most of their residents into halfway houses or unto the streets. But Jason, the adopted son of Jimmy and Ardis Wilcox, would celebrate his twenty-second birthday today, not in Willmar, but in Stillwater.

The lamentable fate so blithely invoked by the names of two Minnesota towns had struck me as I was processed to enter the prison. I had surrendered my driver's license, pushing it under an inch-thick Plexiglas window to a humorless guard. When I had passed through a metal detector, I had to remove my shoes. The young woman noted without comment that my shoes had brass eyelets for the laces. It was clear to me that the rules of behavior that apply at airport security checkpoints also applied here: attempts at joviality were unwelcome. I had made an appointment to see James two weeks in advance. There had been several logbooks to sign; every step was watched with a bored officiousness.

I was only a visiting small-town clergyman come on a small errand of mercy, yet everything was received as suspect, my visit, my shoes, even me. It was, doubtless, a suspicion hardened by experience. If it bears so heavily on a one-hour visitor, how the weight of institution must fall upon inmates. It is not just the bars and electronic security that make a place a prison; it's the waiting. I sat in a visitor holding area for forty minutes, well past the appointed hour to meet James. I had been promised an hour-long face-to-face interview, an indulgence not routinely permitted. But it takes time for a bureaucracy, even a reasonably enlightened one, to bend itself around a small grace.

"Rev. Battles?" asked a guard staring over an open manila folder into my eyes. She looked down at her papers as I looked up to her question. But before I spoke, she turned away and said over her shoulder, "Follow me, please." She led me down a corridor to a small room, eight feet square if that, furnished with a small steel-legged table and two orange fiberglass chairs. "Wait in here, please."

She returned ten minutes later, opened the door, and stepped back. Jason peeked around her into the room and saw me. He smiled shyly, the first smile I had been granted since leaving home at six o'clock that morning. "Fifty minutes," she said. "Knock on the door when you're done." She closed it behind her. The top half was a wire-glass window.

Jason sat down on the chair across the table, laid his hands in his lap, and looked at them. "How are Jimmy and Ardis?" he asked without looking up, "I mean Mom and Dad. Are they okay?"

Ardis and Jimmy Wilcox had adopted the boy when he was a year and a half old, a moon-faced child, silent and distant, who could not yet walk and had long since given up on crying. Ardis had undergone a hysterectomy the first year of their marriage. A suspected ovarian cancer turned out to be severe endometriosis, unusual in a woman so young. Adoption was the only imaginable course toward the parenthood they had always assumed to be in their future. In a laudable fit of altruism, they had agreed to accept an older child, "if he really needs us." They wanted a boy. Jimmy's next older brother, Larry, had never married, and Lamont, the oldest and divorced from Annette, had two daughters. A boy would carry on the name.

The social worker from Lutheran Social Services had visited Ardis and Jimmy, both young and doubtless idealistic, on a fine June day twenty years ago. She had sat on the very lime green couch in the living room from which Ardis had later told me the tale. The social worker described a little boy who really needed them. I know the story in detail because Ardis has told it to me so many times. She always begins by describing the social worker: her seventies dress and coiffure. Then she would place herself and Jimmy in the room and remember the brightness of the day, light pouring in the back window.

"The baby is part Native American, cute little guy. His father died in a car accident up north. The mother has a chronic substance abuse problem and needs to go into a treatment facility in Crookston. So she's decided to give the baby up. She's sure about it. And Mr. and Mrs. Wilcox, it's the right choice for both of them. She's way too young and needs to focus on getting her life straightened around. The baby just turned a year. He's an active little guy, not quite walking. This is a baby that needs you."

She then showed Ardis a snapshot which, as Ardis told the story, she would in turn always hand to me. It was now framed and sits on the end table beside the same lime green couch. Whenever Ardis describes the scene, she ends the narrative by saying, "Nobody said anything about fetal alcohol syndrome. I don't know what they knew back then, maybe nothing, but nobody said a thing."

By the time Jason was five, Ardis had become an authority on fetal alcohol syndrome, "FAS" to the parents, teachers, social workers, therapists, and advocates who have studied its devastations. Ardis told this story to me both because she needed to explain Jason and because she felt duty bound to preach alarm to anyone who would listen: "Heavy drinking, sometimes even moderate drinking, during pregnancy reaches into the brain and the body of a child forming in a womb. Sometimes the effects are minor, barely noticeable if at all. Sometimes they are disastrous. Our Jason has all the scars. They're deep, cut deep into his personality, even into his body."

He now sat across the table from me, small and slight with elfish features. He had lagged behind his peers as a small child. He walked and talked and read late. He had always been veritably impervious to direction. It was not so much that he was defiant as he was enslaved by the moment: bound and obedient to whatever pleased him at the time. He bore discipline only in passing, checked for a time by a scolding or an hour sentenced to his room. But it seemed to bear no lasting impression; in fact little bore a lasting impression on Jason. He was scattered, alternately enthusiastic and then bored. But most disconcerting, he seemed to have little by way of internal moral compass. As a child, he was winsome in an impish sort of way. He coveted approval and acceptance, at first from adults, later from his peers.

It was this latter craving that would lead him to Stillwater. Behavior that had exhausted his parents in childhood turned frightening in early adolescence. By the time he was fifteen, he had run away for the third time and more or less for good. He had hitchhiked north and found his birth mother on the Red Lake Reservation. That summer he had fished Upper Red Lake; come fall he had hunted. Then, with the coming of the short, dark days of winter, he had started to drink with his buddies. His mother recognized this road; she was still on it herself. She loved the boy enough to kick him out of the house and tell him to get off the rez. Ardis had told me that some shocking percentage of FAS kids end up in prison, that they still loved the boy, but had come to accept the hard truth that they could never have heard when they were young, namely, that their love—unbounded and powerful as it might be—could not conquer all. They had been so sure that stubborn constancy and unqualified love would heal this little boy's scars. I doubt that they would have changed their minds about the adoption even if the social worker had spoken of FAS in terrifying detail on that bright June day.

After he left the reservation, Jason had come back to North Haven for a couple of weeks. He stole Jimmy's credit cards and ran off to the Cities. They canceled the cards and heard from the boy every few months. He usually called when he was back on the streets and hungry. They begged him to come home, less insistently as the years wore by, and finally they begged no more. Not that their love was less; they simply hoped for less. Jason had always ached to have friends, but his oddness, even as a small child, usually led him to the worst of companions. In this company of last resort, eager to be approved and with a wandering compass, he stumbled one misstep at a time deeper into trouble. He got caught shoplifting and stealing car radios. Then he stole a couple of cars. "Stumbled" is the better word to describe Jason's fall. Ironically, he is not so much immoral as innocently amoral. He was always the kid who just went along, the kid who happened to be there, and, invariably, the kid who got caught.

He had been the only one of three "alleged perpetrators" to be apprehended after robbing a gas station in Anoka early last fall. When the attendant pulled a gun, the other two had dashed to the car and roared off, leaving Jason to run for it on foot, which he did at a full clip along the shoulder of the road, following his friends in the car. The cops spotted him running toward them as they were roaring to the gas station. He wore his guilt so obviously that he might as well have already been wearing the orange prison uniform he now had on. It was armed robbery, his third felony, and he had just turned twenty-one.

He told the detective that he only knew the first names of his two friends and couldn't remember quite where they lived. This was doubtless the truth, but they didn't believe him. Jason would spend much of his adult life in prison. Sitting there, his odd and childlike face reflected up at me in the shiny Formica top of the tabletop as he looked down, it was painfully obvious that he had come to understand what it all meant. He understood what a long time meant; he had come to comprehend something of the impending inhumanities and humiliations of incarceration. His imagination was able to grasp the future, not firmly enough to have done anything much differently, but firmly enough to be afraid.

"The chaplaincy team, they have Bible studies," he said, looking up at me, warming to a subject that he guessed would please me. "I go every week. We read out loud. I'm gonna keep it up."

I could not tell whether this promise was another manifestation of Jason's unflagging zeal to please or the outside possibility of some spiritual quickening. "Tell Ardis and Jimmy that I'm going to Bible study with the chaplaincy team. Be sure you tell 'em." "Mom and Dad" had become "Ardis and Jimmy" the year he went north.

I found myself carrying most of the conversation: bits of news from North Haven, his Uncle Larry's recovery after the accident out in Nebraska and his photographs. Jason for his part had little to say, mostly news about prison regulations: when he could listen to the radio and when he couldn't, the ham they had for dinner the evening before. I offered up the birthday gift that I had been given to deliver from Ardis and Jimmy. I knew the roughly rewrapped package contained not only the boom box and pile of CDs he had requested, but a pair of mittens Ardis had knit. Their package, as well as the one from his Uncle Larry, had both been opened and thoroughly inspected on the way in. His adoptive parents had visited over Christmas and the experience had devastated Jimmy. They had asked me to go for them on his birthday.

Uncle Larry's gift was one of his photographs, of course, this one looking across the water at a meadow that lies near the narrows of Carthage Lake. For Jason he had chosen this scene over the tumbled-down barns or derelict farmhouses he usually favors.

Every year for years to come, there would be gifts on the thirteenth of May, his birthday, not his adoption day. But what do you give a boy in prison for his birthday? What do you give a man in prison on his thirtieth birthday? How many birthdays would Jason keep in Stillwater, and what would come of him when he finally got out, a man entering middle-age with FAS?

Ardis had told me that some FAS kids make it, but she no longer dared to hope that Jason might fall in that number. Alive and sitting across the table on an orange fiberglass chair, the boy was an incarnation of all the things that cannot be fixed. How could anything good ever be wrestled from the teeth of this beast? All the love Ardis and Jimmy had poured into him had touched him, I am sure. Perhaps their love had somewhat deflected his heedless course, but it was never enough. Jason was Jason. He was the emblem of that which we may fear the most: not evil, not even death, but the terrible truth that love cannot conquer all. Like Jimmy and Ardis, I once struggled to believe that this was not so, namely, that love—faithful enough, deep enough, tireless enough, bottomless love—could not but win. Now I sat in an eight-by-eight room in Stillwater across the table from what looked for all the world to be a loss.

He looked away from the boom box and the matted

photograph and said, "Uncle Lamont sent me a present too." He brightened with the thought of it. "Where is it?" I asked. "I mean, what did he give you?"

"It's up north," he replied. "It's a wolf up north."

My mystified look invited explanation. Jason offered it in words that were surely not all his, many of them gleaned from the letter that Lamont had written, the letter that had borne the gift, a letter that he had obviously read and reread. "Some biologists up north are trying to bring timber wolves back. There haven't been many wolves on the rez for years. And if you make a big enough donation, they name a wolf for you. Uncle Lamont used to live up in Alaska and he, like, respects wolves. He makes pretty good money selling Jet-Skis in Wayzata. Anyway, he made a donation, and my wolf has a tag in its ear that says 'Jason James Wilcox.' Uncle Lamont told me about it in a letter last week. Every night in my bunk bed I think about the wolf. Sometimes I can seen him moving in the woods, in my mind you know. I saw a timber wolf up north once. I was walking a logging trail when I was staying on the rez with my other mom." He hesitated, looked toward the door and then back at me. "And then sometimes, it's like I'm inside of him. I can, like, see what he sees. Sometimes I move through the woods with him at night. I see the white-tails and I spot snowshoe rabbits with him. And I run and I run through the snow. Last night when I was lying in my bunk, it was like I was looking across Upper Red Lake across the ice, just ice as far as I could see."

I drove home in the waning light of late afternoon. I-35 was wet; traffic was heavy around the Cities. The boy's image of transcendence lay in my mind's eye: Jason in his wolf, Jason out of prison, Jason out of his FAS mind, Jason up north, Jason free of it all. But some broken things just cannot be fixed. There are broken people who cannot be healed in this world, neither by our love nor our cleverness. Some cancer patients get better; others don't. Some FAS kids make it; some never will. Some wounded souls heal; some go to their graves pulled into the earth by darkness no mortal love can ever lighten.

Within the walls of time, confined by this mortal space, hemmed in by the limits of our loving and understanding, the truth we hate to know is that all will not be well here. Ardis and Jimmy had come to realize this, finally. But on the other side of these walls, I cannot but hope that there lies another long stretch of truth. In those vast expanses, I cannot but trust there to be some greater loving, some deeper knowing that shall conquer all. I have to trust this. I must hope for a place where it all gets fixed, a place where there is no FAS, no cancer, no Parkinson's, no Willmar, no Stillwater, a place where former things are passed away, all tears are wiped away, a place where there is only up north, only Upper Red Lake seen through the eyes of a wolf on the shore looking over that pure sea of crystal, ice blown clear of snow, a great mirror in the moonlight.

— 11 —

May 26, The Day of Pentecost

Our Organist

This is my commandment, that you love one another as I have loved you.

—John 15:12

When the Minnesota state road map was published this year, the town of Carthage Lake was not there. Nobody from the state highway department wrote to tell the dozen folks who fancied they lived in Carthage Lake, Minnesota, that there was, officially speaking, no longer going to be such a place. North Haven may be withering year by year as are so many of the little towns on the plains, but even our town dwarfs Carthage Lake, which has withered bone-dry: seven weathered frame houses, only five of them inhabited, plus the church. First Presbyterian of Carthage Lake was named, I suppose, in the fond but unfounded hopes of the settlers of the last century that the place would be great enough one day to afford a second. There is no post office, no gas station; there never was a bar.

The last minister left Carthage Lake in 1939. He blew away with the dust bowl and the Depression, and with him went most of the town, but not all. A faithful remnant, fewer and fewer every year, but the more tenacious for their smaller numbers, have saved it from the dread fate of so many country churches: becoming an antique shop, a warehouse of memories for sale, an old church full of rusty saws and wood planes, Admiral radios from the fifties that don't work, stacks of old *National Geographics*. Saddest of all in such places are the old family photos and Bibles. Around here they are often in Swedish or German with the births and deaths noted between the Testaments. They were left behind when the farm was sold and the last grandniece moved to Mankato and didn't think to take them with her.

Come every summer these relics are casually venerated, touched, examined, and sometimes purchased by pilgrims from the Cities, good people from places like Brooklyn Park whose children sit impatiently on the front steps and yell, "Mom!" into the musty dimness of the old church. The father, also inside, picks up an old glossy black and white photo of some big-eyed baby in a sun bonnet staring soberly out of 1921. He touches his wife's arm to show her the photo of the baby. They smile, and he puts the photo back in the box. It's not their child after all, and the frame has a chip in the corner.

It is a stalwart few who hold this fate at bay and keep First Presbyterian of Carthage Lake, still a church with pews where people worship the living God on a Sunday, but not every Sunday anymore. It's only one Sunday a month, and soon I would guess, it will be every other month, and then after a few funerals, the pews and the two stained-glass windows will be auctioned off, and maybe an antique dealer will buy the building for his shop. But for a while yet, a visiting minister comes once a month, usually a visiting minister who has already preached his sermon that morning to his own congregation and has been cajoled by Lloyd Larson to preach it again at noon in Carthage Lake to the eleven souls who will always be there barring bad colds or worse than usual rheumatism. Lloyd has been the clerk of session for the last thirty-one years, and when he calls, he always says, "Yep, dere ain't so many of us no more, but you'll have 100 percent attendance, Preacher."

I was invited to preach at Carthage Lake this last Sunday, my second invitation in the last ten years. I had turned the first one down because Annie's family was in town for the week. North Haven is a good fifty miles from Carthage Lake, a fast dash on Minnesota backroads in the hour between our service and theirs. It was Tuesday morning early when Lloyd called looking for a preacher for the Sunday coming, the Day of Pentecost. A whisper of desperation leaked from his practiced bonhomie. He offered the same confession and same promise as he had offered when he had called five or six years ago: a small group, but a faithful one. And he promised me an organist, the same organist he promised the last time, the same organist Carthage Lake had been promising guest preachers for the last sixty years: Lloyd's sister-in-law, Agnes Rigstad.

I said I'd be pleased to preach in Carthage Lake, but cautioned him that I might be a little late arriving.

Lloyd said late was fine; they'd wait church on me. Next morning I called back to give him the title of the sermon and the hymns for Agnes. No answer and no answering machine; octogenarians by some shared wisdom never seem to have answering machines. I asked Maureen, our volunteer church secretary, to try again later, or maybe just drop him a note with the hymns and the sermon title.

Come Sunday, I arrived late, five minutes after noon, that being the odd hour at which once-a-month church has been scheduled these last decades for the benefit of preachers doing second shift. The church was a white frame building, freshly painted with a truncated mock-Norman tower in one corner. On the walls to either side of the steeple were two large and sentimental stained-glass windows: one of Jesus the Good Shepherd, lamb in one arm, staff in the other; the second showed Jesus praying alone in the Garden of Gethsemane, his eyes lifted toward heaven. There were two cars and a pickup in front of the church. I assumed that most of the eleven worshipers rumored to be present every Sunday had walked.

Inside there were twelve people, all but Lloyd seated in the front two pews of the little Akron-style sanctuary. Lloyd, whom I recognized from the presbytery meetings he doggedly attended on behalf of "Carthage Lake First," was standing beneath the pulpit in the far corner. At eighty years, he was perhaps the youngest of the congregation save one, a young man sitting at the end of the second pew. Lloyd was slowly reading the denomination's adult-education program leader's guide to the others who were listening attentively as the old man worked to breathe life to stiff, didactic prose that outlined the development of medieval, Reformation, and modern theories of the atonement. He was just finishing reading through the discussion questions, all five straight through without a pause for response in between. This, clearly, was the adult Sunday school class.

"Well, that's that, then," he said, closing the guide. "Next week we do the Trinity. Hello, Reverend, perfect timing."

The class stood up slowly, all except the young man, and moved to what I assumed were their accustomed places for worship, stations to which they had habituated themselves decades ago when the sanctuary might have been half full. But now, numbers thinned by moves and death, they were oddly scattered about the room. One very old lady in what was obviously a wig slightly askew on her head mounted the chancel steps and went to the organ bench to the right of the pulpit. She looked my way and presented me with a broad and surprisingly toothy smile. Lloyd pulled me over and offered the same *sotto voce* instructions he had given a hundred visiting ministers before me: talk loud, there's no mike and some folks don't hear as well as they used to. As Lloyd whispered this instruction into my face with coffee breath, I could not but notice one elderly couple settling into the very back pew.

Doubtless the deafest of the lot, I thought to myself. They always sit in back.

Then Lloyd added, "And we don't do a Sunday bulletin no more. Can't get parts for the Gestetner, so you just gotta tell us when it's time for a hymn."

With that Lloyd made a grand sweeping gesture to the heavy carved mahogany chair behind the pulpit with a padded seat of burgundy velvet. Then he went to the second pew and sat next to the young man.

I prayed silently before I stood to speak the call to worship, prayed for dwindling flocks and their shepherds. Then I stood and said, "This is the day the Lord has made; let us rejoice and be glad in it. Let us join together in singing hymn number 204." I glanced over to Agnes to make sure she had heard this last. She smiled back her gleaming smile and launched into the hymn. She had not played but a measure before I realized that she was not playing "Spirit of God, Descend upon My Heart." It took me another moment to recognize "What a Friend We Have in Jesus." I furrowed my brow and stood up well after the little congregation had risen to sing. They sang well for eleven old people and one young man. He was the only one with a hymnal in his hand; the others were clearly singing from memory. Maybe Agnes didn't hear, I whispered to myself.

I read the New Testament lesson in a voice that was just an inch this side of a shout. The Pentecost text was some of Jesus' many words from John's Gospel, words that he spoke to his little band of followers on the eve of his death. John records an extraordinary number of last words, about five chapters' worth. They include Jesus' promise to send the Holy Spirit, the "Counselor," that Pentecost protagonist. "I will not leave you desolate," John's Jesus promises them.

I also read some words from the next chapter as well, Jesus' injunction—spoken several times almost as a fond wish—that his followers might love one another after he was gone: "This is my commandment, that you love one another as I have loved you." Not exactly Pentecost words, but they seemed fit words for both North Haven and Carthage Lake, little bands of disciples as beleaguered as that first one, alone in a place on the cusp of desolate. Nobody to love them but Jesus and each other. This is what I said in the sermon, more or less, a teachy sermon about the Johannine community for which the Gospel was written, a sermon about love and the power of the Spirit abiding among those who love each other well.

But as I preached I must confess that love was more on my lips than in my heart. After reading the scripture and before preaching the sermon, I had announced the middle hymn, "Love Divine, All Love Excelling," a hymn that I had carefully chosen for this sermon. I announced it very loudly and rather too pointedly, looking Agnes in the eyes. She smiled back before diving at the organ keys and launching into "I Love to Tell the Story."

After the sermon I prayed, prayed for the old and the sick especially, as well as the young and confused. I prayed for this bewildered world and I prayed for Carthage Lake. Having prayed some of this once before that day, I found my soul taking a detour from the prayer notes on my yellow legal pad. My detoured but unspoken prayer, floating above my leaden words was more of a cry than Presbyterians usually permit themselves: *Why, O God, why?* my heart wandered. *Week after week, we come to you with these same prayers, the same words plus or minus, again and again. We pray for peace and get more of the Middle East. We pray for health and greet death. We pray out our hopes and yet we wither. Why?*

When it came time to announce the last hymn, I looked at Agnes and thought better of it. I took two steps over to the organ bench, bent down, and whispered loudly in her ear, "Agnes, what are we going to sing?" She smiled her denture grin, said not a word, and began to play "Just As I Am, without One Plea."

After the service was over I greeted at the door. Agnes smiled broadly as she pumped my hand, but said nothing beyond, "Nice sermon, Reverend." Lloyd and the young man were at the front of the church when I went back to gather up my notes. Lloyd gave me a sheepish look, the young man a knowing glance that recognized my chagrin.

Lloyd spoke quickly to get the first word: "Forgot to tell you about Agnes," he said. "You don't need to tell us what the hymn is, only when. Agnes only knows those three hymns, so we always sing 'em."

"How long has she been your organist?" I asked, my voice rising with the question.

"Well," Lloyd looked down at the worn carpet at the foot of the pulpit, "since '37 when old Rev. Simmons left . . . Old," Lloyd added mostly to himself, "he was probably forty when he left town, but I was only twenty-three. It's all perspective, hey, Dave? Anyhoo, Rev. Simmons's wife, she played the organ for us back then, and when she was gone, there was nobody. So Agnes learned to play."

"Good God, Lloyd, you mean to tell me you've been singing the same three hymns every month for sixty years!"

He was concentrating on the carpet more intently. "We like those hymns well enough, and we know 'em by heart." And then he raised his eyes from the floor and met mine. He said, almost defiantly, "and she is our organist. You want some coffee, Reverend? I got a Thermos out in the truck."

He disappeared out the door and across the road to a rusty brown Ford pickup. The young man advanced into my bewildered silence, and offered a hand and a deliberately strong grip.

"My name is Neil Larson. I'm Lloyd's grandson, I've been living with him for the last few months. Moved up here from Texas in March. You have to understand about Agnes. She's my late grandmother's little sister, Lloyd's wife's baby sister. Agnes has never been quite right. 'Don't have both oars in the water,' is the way Lloyd puts it. He means it kindly. She never says more than a few words, and usually the same words. But she learned to play those three hymns in one week sixty years ago. It was a moment of musical emergency. Anyway, she hasn't been able to learn another one since. Playing the organ this one Sunday a month means the world to her. Sometimes I think it's mostly for her that they keep the church open. Aunt Agnes lives for the first Sunday of the month."

We both watched as Neil played with the frayed carpet with the toe of his brown penny loafer. Lloyd was standing in the doorway of the church with a Thermos and some paper cups, letting Neil talk to me alone.

"They asked me to play, of course. They had to ask. But Grandpa knew I'd say no when he asked. I remember how he sighed with relief when I said no. Then he slapped me on the back."

"You're an organist?" I asked.

"Eastman, class of '84. I've had some big church jobs, the last one down in Texas, big Baptist church in the Houston 'burbs. Brand new Cassavant, 102 ranks. Four services a Sunday. Then I got sick. I've been HIV positive for six years, but it wasn't till last fall that I got sick. The personnel committee of the church figured it out, the weight loss, all the sick days, not married. They told me it would be best if I were to move on, but not till after Christmas, of course. My parents live in St. Paul, but my father and I haven't spoken since I was nineteen. I'm on the cocktail, not sick enough for the hospital, but I'm just too tired most of the time to work. I actually had nowhere to go. My grandfather said I could move in with him and Agnes. To tell the truth I kinda feel right at home in a town of eighty-year-olds."

He looked up from the carpet, held my eyes, and said,

"You know, Pastor, that was a fine sermon, but I think that they got it a while ago. I think they'd heard already, I mean the 'love one another' part. And they have not been left desolate."

He paused and went on, "They keep Agnes, and they took me in. And since I moved up here, most every night either Lloyd or old man Engstrom from down the road opens up the church for me. If it's cold they lay a fire in the woodstove. And then I play the organ. It's a sweet little instrument, believe it or not. Lloyd's kept it up. These last weeks, it's been almost warm in the evenings, so they leave the doors and the windows of the church open and everybody sits out on their front porch and they listen to me play, Bach, Buxtehude, Widor, Ruger, all the stuff I love. And they clap from their porches, even Agnes claps."

— 12 —

May 30, Memorial Day

Thin Wine

Your silver has become dross,
and your wine mixed with water.
—Isaiah 1:22

Memorial Day parades have grown shorter and fewer with the years between us and the wars we would sooner remember, those two numbered ones, blessed as they were with some moral clarity. North Haven's own parade had become embarrassingly short by the early eighties and was finally discontinued. After it was halted, Memorial Day was reduced to the ceremony that used to follow the parade itself: readings of "The Gettysburg Address" and "In Flanders' Fields" in front of the GAR Memorial next to the church. Until the high school closed, the two readers were always the two top senior students, the valedictorian reading Lincoln, the salutatorian reading McCray.

After the readings, the oldest ambulatory North Haven veteran stepped forward and laid a floral wreath at the foot of the memorial. Even as late as 1941, I have been told, it was a Civil War veteran who performed this honor, some grizzled member of the local chapter of the Grand Army of the Republic. Through the next five decades, a sequence of North Haven veterans of the Great War laid the wreath. In more recent years, one of several dozen World War II vets in town stepped forward after hearing yet again how poppies grow ("row on row") and solemnly placed the ring of red and white carnations dressed with a ribbon of blue at the foot of the ten-foot Minnesota granite obelisk. He would then salute stiffly while some high school kid, for a while Danny Olson, more recently his little sister, Tiffany, did their best with "Taps." Last May, after several years of awkwardly sparse attendance, even this truncated remembrance was laid to rest.

So this past Monday Annie and the kids and I drove up to Redwood Falls for their Memorial Day parade.

We were inspired less by patriotism and more by the fact that our older child was marching with her band. Jennifer plays the clarinet just well enough to make the Sleepy Eye Regional High School Marching Band, which was slated to be one of several attractions in a reinvigorated parade in Redwood Falls. Parade time, noted the flyer that went out to all band parents, was ten. Band members, however, had been asked to report to the park where the parade was to line up an hour earlier. We arrived just before nine, both in order to get Jen to the park and to secure prime curbside viewing real estate for her blindly supportive family. Annie is five months pregnant, showing and feeling well enough, but we brought along a folding lawn chair to keep her off of her feet.

So it was the three of us, Annie, me and Chris, who just turned thirteen and is suddenly loathe to be seen in the proximity of his parents in public. We need not have worried about arriving early enough to get a spot on the curb. The parade route was empty, save for scattered knots of early arrivals who looked to be parents of other clarinetists and trombone players. Much of the route was marked by yellow plastic bags labeled "No Parking" that shrouded parking meters.

We secured what looked to be a desirable stretch of curb directly in front of a towering red brick church at a conspicuous intersection where one might expect bands to make a point of playing. We parked the Taurus in back of the church in an unmarked gravel lot with no signs that forbade doing so and found our way around the side to the front of the building. It was an ambitiously large edifice, built, I guessed, at the turn of the nineteenth century in the then-fashionable red-brick Gothic style. I noted that the brickwork needed to be tuck-pointed sooner rather than later. The small lawn had been recently mowed, but the foundation plantings were overgrown. The place had an air of disuse about it. I looked, but there was no sign to identify the congregation.

I unfolded the aluminum chair, into which Annie was not yet ready to settle, and we each glanced at our watches: nine-fifteen. The parade officially started half a mile up the street at ten. Officially, that is. In practice, parades seldom begin on time. Christopher muttered, "They're not going be coming by here for at least another *hour.*" He then sighed as he rolled his eyes and ambled far enough away from his mother and me so that any other thirteen-year-old who might see him would never guess that he even knew these embarrassing adults who only happened to look like him.

Annie and I wandered off in search of coffee, quite unnecessarily leaving the chair in place to mark our piece of curb. Chris lagged about twenty feet behind, just far enough back that he might appear to be in Redwood Falls on a Saturday morning quite on his own. When we returned, there was a thin and broken line of parade watchers, all toes to the curb and gazing up the street with mild anticipation.

It was not a long parade, perhaps thirty minutes of patriotism mixed with Americana, assorted curiosities, anachronism, and advertisement. "Jennifer's band," as we name it, led the parade and did indeed play Souza most credibly at our very intersection. Christopher sang the words loudly for all to hear: "Be kind to your friends in the swamp, for a duck may be somebody's mother."

There were several VFW color guard units from the surviving posts in Brown and Redwood Counties. Young soldiers they were not. There was but one float, a hand-me-down from recent Fourth of July parades sponsored by a coalition of local service clubs. Atop a flatbed trailer pulled by an immense black four-wheel-drive pickup, a six-foot papier-mâché Statue of Liberty, painted a livid green and trembling as she lumbered along, raised her torch from the peak of what seemed to be a mountain rising out of the trailer. The gold-lettered caption over the tinsel fringe around the circumference of the trailer read, "America Means Progress and Prosperity." Down the sides of her mountain were littered assorted emblems of Miss Liberty's prosperity and progress: small appliances of various kinds, microwaves, CD players, VCRs, toy representations of autos, trucks, tractors, and a model of a split-level home doubtless purloined from some Jaycee's model railroad display.

That most esoteric of veterans' organizations, *40 Hommes et 8 Cheveaux,* was represented by seven, not forty, very old men waving languidly not from eight horses, but from two benches set on the bed of a late-thirties Ford flatbed truck. Next came the Redwood

Falls High School Marching Band in sleek uniforms and playing a medley of Broadway show tunes. There were a dozen antique autos, their owners' wives and grandchildren waving proudly from the open windows. I noted with some chagrin that two of them were models of automobiles I had once owned, though not quite when they were new. Of course, the final punctuation, always the period at the end of the sentence of any parade, was a local equestrian club, in this case the Redwood County Palominos. Christopher screwed up his nose and uttered a two-syllable "gah-ross" as the last of the palominos, a magnificent stallion, choose to relieve himself not twenty feet from us.

But the most curious of all parade curiosities and surely the most memorable of memorial memories passed by at the very center of the parade, just after our own North Haven VFW Color Guard. We heard them before we saw them, the roar of many engines being gunned in sync, an impressive if not ominous tenor to the patented bass Harley-Davidson roar. They lurched down the street toward us, twelve, fourteen, twenty, twenty-four Honda three-wheeled ATVs—all terrain vehicles. They were identical, all of them painted flame red and driven by men, mostly in their sixties and seventies, in shiny gold pants, shimmering white shirts, and white patent-leather shoes. Each had a red fez on his head. Their leader held up his hand and they stopped with uncanny precision directly before us. Written in gold sequins on the front of each fez were the words: "Temple of Saladin." Below the words was a sequin outline of a sword, broad and curved in the Moorish style. Each driver wore sunglasses and had a two-way radio with earphones and a microphone fitted before his deadly earnest mouth. Strapped behind most of the drivers was a teddy bear, riding backward. The lead Honda had a sign mounted to the rear of the driver and next to his baby-blue and white teddy bear. It identified him and his brothers as the "Saladin Shrine Precision-Driving ATV Team."

I saw the leader speak into his microphone, lower his head, then raise his left hand to heaven, only to drop it forward, pointing menacingly down Main Street, a Minnesota chevalier leading his fellow knights into the fray. This time, they did not simply roar forward in formation, but embarked upon the most studied and intricate series of maneuvers: figure-eights, concentric circles, then a tandem inner formation of two rows heading down the street while the two outer lines came back up the street, all finally wheeling around to form themselves into some new mobile intricacy.

Sometimes they would turn sharply enough to bring their three-wheeled steeds up on two wheels, eliciting gasps and applause from the crowd. It was orchestrated with marching-band precision, but executed at twenty miles per hour by old men with teddy bears. All this was done without a hint of a smile crossing a single Shriner's face. They ended where they started, just before us. The leader again spoke into his microphone, raised his left hand, and pointed down the Main Street of Redwood Falls. Transmissions in neutral, they roared their idling engines, found first gear, executed two-dozen uniform but cautious wheelies, and advanced.

Behind them irony hung as thick as their cloud of blue two-cycle smoke. These were Shriners, an American manifestation of Scottish Freemasonry, that secret society which had emerged at the end of the Middles Ages. Freemasons had first given themselves out to be the heirs of medieval guilds of stonemasons who had possessed arcane secrets, sacred geometry, and brotherly virtues. Their knowledge and their rites, so they hinted, could be traced back to the building of Solomon's Temple and the king's architect, Hiram Abiff. This obscure history was much on my mind, as I had just finished a book on the subject, a reading occasioned by a rather sensational program on Freemasonry that I had watched on the History Channel the middle of one sleepless night.

Many scholars argue that the origins of Freemasonry actually lay in the Knights Templar, that famous and infamous order of monkish knights formed in 1118, the opening years of the Crusades, by a French nobleman named Hugues de Payen. Like all monks, they swore oaths of poverty, chastity, and obedience. Unlike any others, they were also a military order, fierce warriors, who pledged never to surrender unless the odds were worse than three to one. Initiates yielded all land and wealth to the order upon joining. Supported by no less than Bernard of Clairvaux, they were recognized by the Council of Troyes and undertook their central task: to provide safe passage to pilgrims visiting Crusader-occupied Jerusalem. They soon became a force to be reckoned with, both in the Middle East and in Europe. They were fascinated with the Holy Grail, the Ark of the covenant, and the mount on which the Temple had stood, which they ultimately made their headquarters.

Templar wealth and power grew enormous. At the end of the Crusades, when the last Europeans were expelled from the Holy Land, they focused their clandestine energies on Europe. They raised castles across the continent and were behind the building of the greatest medieval cathedrals, most notably Chartres. But brutish rumors flew, especially among jealous princes and popes, rumors of heresy and sexual license. Their fall came at the hands of that most jealous of kings, Philip the Fair of France, who banned the order, convinced the pope to excommunicate them, and slowly roasted the last grand master, Jacques de Molay, over a spit in the shadow of Notre Dame.

But many say that Templar rites and knowledge were passed on to others, notably Freemasons, who in their own time became a force to be reckoned with. Freemasons, mixing alchemy with science, were behind the founding of England's Royal Society, that cradle of modern scientific thought. Their numbers included fathers of science, art, and democracy, the likes of Francis Bacon, Isaac Newton, Mozart, and George Washington. In more modern times, they became leaders of philanthropy and the champions of sick children. In these latter days, whatever the truth may have been, most Masons gladly owned the heritage of the Templars, naming their lodges "temples" and calling their order for boys after their martyr, de Molay.

But now, in Redwood Falls, Minnesota, all these years later, it had all come down to this: two dozen old men on three-wheel motor scooters. In some monumental historical confusion, Moorish fezzes and oriental swords had become friendly emblems, and in an ultimate obfuscation, these putative heirs of Templars took the very name of Saladin, the Kurdish warlord who had driven them out of the Holy Land, perhaps the only name they despised as much as that of Philip the Fair.

As they roared off I thought to myself, *How it all erodes: the alchemy-science of Freemasonry is reduced to mixing gasoline and oil in the right ratio for two-cycle engines. How it all withers: the sacred geometry of Chartres and Rosslyn Chapel is reduced to diagrams for precision ATV driving. How lofty things can collapse inward: the Templar oath of poverty, chastity, and obedience becomes a promise to make three of the four annual parades.*

I could not shake the jolting juxtaposition of images, the Templars mounted on their armored stallions and these doubtless good-hearted Shriners mounted on their three-wheeled Japanese steeds. I smiled, but sadly, at the irony of it. Annie, now standing, yanked me from my musings, "David, what's so funny?"

"Nothing, nothing's funny," a little domestic lie to cover a story too long to tell right then. I picked up the aluminum chair and we followed Chris, who had disappeared around the back of the church a half an hour earlier to sit in the car after his sister's band had passed by.

At a smaller door into the towering church building, to the side and not the main entrance, a man in dark blue shirt and pants leaned against an open doorway smoking a cigarette. As we passed by, I asked him, "What's the name of the church?"

"Trinity," he answered, dropping the cigarette and grinding it into the sidewalk with the toe of his black work boot.

"What denomination is it?" I asked.

"*'Was,'* you mean. I dunno." He stood away from the doorway and grew suddenly loquacious. "They pay me to come in a couple of hours each day to keep the place looking half decent and to keep the pipes from freezing up in the winter. They don't have church here no more. They're trying to sell the place, but nobody wants it. Too big. But there's some endowment money to pay me and the oil bills."

"It's a gorgeous building," I said as I looked up again at the twin red-brick Gothic spires.

"You want to see inside," he asked, obviously bored with his job.

I looked at Annie, who said, "Chris and I will pick up Jennifer and be back here in half an hour."

"I'm Curt," the caretaker said, extending a hand. "Never was their actual janitor. Never worked here when it was a going operation. It's something to see though. Watch your step, it's dark inside. No reason to replace all the lightbulbs."

He led me through a maze of dark and winding corridors to a door that opened into the front of the sanctuary. There he stopped and said, "Let me get the lights, what lights there are."

The sanctuary was an awe-full exercise in late Victorian indulgence. They loved all things medieval, our great-grandparents, they created this sacred space to evoke the Gothic as best as they could without spending the extra for stone. The windows to each side were in three sets of three, each tipped with a pointed arch. At the back, high over the street, was a great gray circle where a rose window had once been. I now noticed that all the windows had been removed and replaced with painted plywood set inside the tracery.

"They sold the windows a good ten years ago; that's where a lot of the money came from. I hear they were something, those windows; told the whole Bible story, I mean from the Garden of Eden on." Then he turned around and pointed to the front of the vast room into the deep chancel, "And after that, they sold off the cross and the communion stuff, all pure silver you know. It was worth a fortune. They say the cross was a beautiful thing."

He leaned his rear against an intricately carved mahogany pew end. "The wife and I used to come over here for their chicken dinners on Fridays. This place was famous for its Friday night dinners. In fact, that's about all they were famous for. Four-bucks-a-head-all-you-can-eat back then. Two bucks for kids under twelve, the chicken dinners. That, and they sold church plates. Never sold 'em all, though. Two boxes down in the basement. You want one? Don't know much else about the place, what they did or anything. Nobody seems to remember much what they did."

I declined a church plate, and Curt led me back through the labyrinthine corridors and into the bright late morning. As I stood on the sidewalk waiting for Annie and the kids, I could not but mourn all lofty things that fall inward, falling so incrementally as to collapse unnoticed. The medieval Order of the Knights Templar becomes, an inch at a time, an ATV precision-driving team, and no one notices. The Way of the Crucified One becomes, an inch at a time, Trinity Church, famous for Friday-night chicken suppers and commemorative plates, and no one notices. As I looked down the street for Annie, I swore I could still see the blue haze of two-cycle ATV smoke hanging in the air above what had once been a church.

— 13 —

June 14

Mama Killdeer

How often would I have gathered your children together as a hen gathers her brood under her wing, and you would not!

—Matthew 23:37

Larry and Sherry MacDowell and their three children, now eleven, nine, and seven, flew out from Spokane last month to be with Minnie for Mother's Day. They pulled into the gravel driveway late Saturday afternoon in a minivan rented at the Minneapolis-St. Paul International Airport. I was on the MacDowells' front porch as they arrived and saw all four of the van's doors burst open at once, the three kids exploding out of the rear two. *Four hours on the plane, three in airports, two and a half in the van,* I thought. Skip, the youngest, had stumbled out last and fell to his knees in the grass beside the driveway. With the lightning-fast reflexes of a seven-year-old, he grabbed his older sister by both ankles and brought her down, thereby keeping things even. As the kids clambered up the front porch and past me, Larry and Sherry sat in their seats with the front doors open, savoring silence and anxious, I imagined, about the days to come.

Donnie, the younger of Minnie's two sons, had called from California Sunday after church. He was sorry that he couldn't make it, but weekends were super-busy at the store and he was having trouble getting help. At least he called; many years he had not bothered. Larry, on the other hand, always phoned the second Sunday in May, and this year he had come in the flesh with his wife and brood. Angus had not told him how ill his mother was. The old man's response to his sons' queries after their mother's health was liturgically predictable: "Maybe a little better." This was not so much a lie as it was reluctance to speak about anything except "a little better." But Angus was afraid. I knew him well enough to hear it in the spaces between his sparse words, but he had no words for such a fear. Had he even possessed them, he would hardly have spoken them. To speak of anything grants it space in the world. Words incarnate—we know this—and the old man wished to invite nothing save "a little better" into Minnie's delicate parlor. She had come home from Brook View the second week in April. Angus waited on her as faithfully as his ninety-one years allowed. A visiting nurse stopped in every other day. Tina Corey, James's mother, had volunteered to clean and do laundry every Saturday, a kindness she offered without comment about the place Angus and Minnie had come to occupy in her son's life.

Three active MacDowell grandchildren utterly displaced James Corey that weekend. Angus later told me that the child had spent all of Mother's Day watching television with his mother and his own grandmother. He had not stopped over even once. James is ill-at-ease with other children; they immediately recognize his strangeness and are less given to circumspection than most adults. He stayed away from the MacDowell house most of the next week as well, even after the hoard of rivals had shoved their way into the Plymouth Voyager and back to Washington State where they belonged.

Children who stand on the outside often learn to watch. Perhaps they have little choice. James, I have come to know, often sees things most children would miss. If the child isn't talking, which is much of the time, he is either listening or watching. His nearly perpetual motion is suddenly stilled as concentration shifts from the making of his surfeit of words to precocious and intense observation of some random oddment of life that might demand his attention.

This last Wednesday, as he would soon tell me, he had seen one such oddment. Thursday, he had gone after school to watch it again. He had been late getting to Angus and Minnie's house, missing the whole Munsters show. Friday he had gone to look again and had not made his routine afternoon stop at the MacDowells' house at all. He had told Angus about what he had found, he later informed me, but Angus would not leave Minnie to come look.

So this morning, a Saturday, James wandered into the church and poked his head around the half-open door of my study. His hair had not been cut for some weeks and was sticking up even more disconcertingly than it usually did. It gave the child an eternally surprised countenance, as though he had just witnessed some electrifying event.

"Dave," he whispered unnecessarily, "I got something to show you." This familiar use of my first name was in imitation of Angus, and more recently Minnie, not the other children of the church. They had finally settled on "Pastor Dave." "You gotta see it," he went on in a conspiratorial whisper. "You're always talking about Jesus-loves-me stuff, so you gotta see this."

"James," I answered, "can it wait till later? I've got so much to do. What is it, anyway?"

"It's something," he responded, deliberately cryptic. "She's there, so you gotta come now. I saw her on the way over."

He was through the door now and had come around my desk. He had me by the hand, tugging insistently. "Later might be too late," he said.

That, I thought, *is often true.* Besides, I knew it would be entirely vain to refuse a focused James Corey. I glanced at the sermon scattered about my desk, giant red-pencil X's having edited out a pair of memorable but irrelevant illustrations. It would now be no more than ten minutes long. Short, I thought, the mantra of my seminary homiletics professor echoing yet again in my memory. "Sermonettes make Christianettes," he had said of any student sermon of less than eighteen minutes.

The Scripture text I was laboring with was one of

those scandalously brief and direct sermons from the Acts of the Apostles that fill the Sundays after Pentecost, these annual days of pretending to be the early church. Peter preaches, then Paul, and both of them with remarkable brevity and directness. This particular sermon was typically terse, an unapologetic presentation of the Jesus who "did not hesitate" to give his life up for the world he loved. By any reckoning it was a sermonette in length, though it seems not to have made for Christianettes. Since the Old Pharisee first preached it, it has been repreached by a million other preachers, and I had the gall to try it again. I let James pull me from my chair.

"Okay, kiddo, let's see what there is to see."

He dropped my hand and raced out of my study and toward the side door of the church. He stopped in the parking lot, turned back to see me emerge onto the steps and said, "Follow me, Dave!" His unbounded enthusiasm had him skipping ten paces ahead of me, stopping, turning, and walking backward until I nearly caught up, then racing ahead again. We walked to his own street, Monroe, turned, and went down past the MacDowell place, then past the little asbestos-shingled bungalow where he and his mother and grandmother lived.

"She's at the end of the street," he whispered loudly. "You gotta sneak up, and you gotta be quiet, Dave. Super quiet."

The street ends at the edge of a soybean field, by mid-June a sea of green, the plants in the irrigated field grown full enough to hide the black loam underneath. Between the soybean field and the last house on the block, a vacant thirties rambler with a rusty metal "For Sale" sign listing in the front yard, there is a large side yard, little tended, though it had been mowed by somebody earlier in the month. James had slowed his pace and was now at my side. He slid his hand into mine and was leading me toward the empty lot. He put his pointer finger to his lips, tapping them twice to keep me quiet. *How many times has this kid seen that gesture aimed at him?* I thought to myself. He led me about fifteen feet into the lot and lay down on his belly in the low grass, motioning me to do the same.

He rested his chin on the palms of both hands and looked into the grass in front of us. Then he turned to me and smiled broadly, certain that I saw what he saw. I gave him an uncomprehending look and silently mouthed the same question I had asked at church, "What is it?" He took a hand from under his chin and pointed, jabbing his finger at some spot in the grass not far in front of us. At first I saw nothing. It had been dangerously dry the first weeks of June, and the grass, even the quack grass and patches of clover in this unwatered lot, were short and turning brown. I strained to see what the child saw, combing the parched grass in front of us toward which James was still jabbing his finger. Then I saw her, a killdeer settled on her nest, stock-still, watching us in the sideways manner of birds.

"It's just a momma killdeer, James," I whispered. "They're all over the place."

Killdeer are smallish ground birds, robin-sized, but much leaner, with long, sticklike legs. They are black and dirty-white on the bellies and cinnamon-brown on their backs, pretty little things with a gratuitous necklace of white and black bands about their necks. They nest in June, oddly choosing open fields for their home, and lay their white-and-gray-specked eggs—three, four, maybe five—out in the open where anyone can see them. The females sit guard for about three weeks and then disappear with their chicks soon after they hatch. But being so readily seen, even in the dry grass camouflage that had hidden this one from my eyes, they can see any approaching enemy; just as this mother had seen James and me. We lay still, watching for a moment.

Suddenly James whispered to me, "Now watch this, Dave. This is the thing you gotta see."

He crept closer on his elbows and knees, his butt sticking up in the air waddling to and fro as he advanced. When he was perhaps ten feet from the nest, he suddenly leapt to his feet and began to wave his arms wildly, crying "Wooo, wooo, hey mama, here I am!"

The killdeer left her nest, sounding the alarm with much frantic cheeping. She moved rapidly toward James, and then away from him and from her eggs. And then she began to do what I had been told killdeer do. I had never seen it, never bothered to look long enough, I suppose. With even louder and more frenetic cheeping, she began to play the cripple, limping pathetically about the field. Feigning a broken wing, she moved toward James, the enemy of her children, and then away, trying to lead him from her eggs. A credible theater this was, one that said, "Take me, I'm an easy mark, fatter than my babies. Here I am, come for me."

James, no longer mindful of stealth, turned to me and called out in full voice, "You know what, Dave? She's not hurt at all. Her wing isn't broke or nothing. She's just pretending. Angus says she does that so I'll go after her and get her, and then her babies will be safe. Isn't that something, Dave? Isn't that something?"

He came back to where I still lay watching and lay back down beside me in the coarse grass, his chin cupped again in his hands, waiting for the mama killdeer to return as he knew she would. "Do you think all mothers would do that for their babies?" he asked without looking at me.

It was not precisely the question he wanted an answer for. It was not "all mothers" that James Corey wondered about.

"I don't know about all mothers, but I bet your mom would," I said, glancing to him to see how he would receive my judgment.

It was the answer I had to give, though I was less than confident it was the truth. Tina Corey is so young to be mother to this awkward little boy. She doubtless loves her fatherless son, perhaps tenaciously, but often sloppily. She is away too much, and too often tired, and cares nothing for BB guns or Legos or the rigors of second-grade spelling lists. Angus and Minnie are picking up the slack, which Tina understands. She vacuums and mops her unspoken appreciation every Saturday morning. Work is the articulation of her love, five days a week at the Holiday Inn and Saturdays at the MacDowells' house, an oversized Victorian that Minnie can no longer keep to within a hair's breath of God's own perfection.

"You think Minnie would do that for those three kids from Spokane?" he asked, as though the question were still at a distance from him.

"I suppose so," I answered. We lay still and waited until this mama came back to the four speckled eggs we had counted in her nest. She still eyed us warily, but settled back down, keeping one glassy little black eye cocked our way.

As I lay there in the warm late morning sun watching her with James, I remembered something Annie had read aloud in the car just after Christmas. We had been driving home to Pennsylvania to spend the week between Sundays with my parents. She had bought one of those cheery holiday magazines in a service area on the Ohio Turnpike and found an article suggesting an ambitious decorating theme built around the old carol, "The Twelve Days of Christmas." The project was utterly unrealistic and would have demanded an entire paid staff of assistant Christmas decorators to pull it off. But more interestingly, each suggested project was accompanied by a brazenly theological gloss expounding on the meaning of each of the twelve sets of gifts offered in the song by the lover to his true love. I had always assumed that they were no more than arbitrary extravagances. Who, after all, would present his true love with six geese on the thirty-first of December?

"They each mean something, I mean something religious," she had said. "It's all a grand allegory set in the twelve days between Christmas and Epiphany."

"The *twelve drummers drumming,*" I remembered her reading, "are the twelve doctrines of the Creed." I had never counted.

"Not the twelve apostles?" I had queried.

"No, they're the *eleven pipers piping,* twelve minus Judas."

It turned into a car game for the next few miles, the kids removing their Walkman earphones and playing along. We guessed as best we could at the allegorical significance of each odd gift. You could not but be intrigued, as you are when something that has long been an unnoticed piece of life's furniture is suddenly declared a valuable antique.

And now, these six months later as I lay on my stomach in dry prickly grass beside James, oddly silent and intent in the June sun, I worked my memory down through the twelve gifts. The *ten lords a-leaping*. . . . Christopher had guessed it: "The Ten Commandments? No-brainer," he had pronounced. The *nine ladies dancing* were Paul's list of nine fruits of the Holy Spirit; the *eight maids a-milking* were Jesus' beatitudes from the Sermon on the Mount. The *seven swans a-swimming* turned out to be yet another list of spiritual gifts. None of these last did we hit upon. The *six geese a-laying* were the six days of creation. I had guessed that. The *five golden rings* were none other than the Torah, the first five books of the Old Testament. The *four calling birds* were the Gospels. We called that one out in unison. The *three French hens* were the Trinity, just as easy. The *two turtle doves* were the Old and New Testaments, which stumped us all.

Neither could we guess the lone *partridge in a pear tree.* Annie had to read it to us. "The pear tree," she had read in florid holiday magazine prose that now came back to me, "The pear tree is a heavenly apple, rare and sweet, celestial counterpart to the red apple, which fruit had brought Eden low when it nourished the First Adam with forbidden fruit. And the partridge," Annie had read, "the partridge hen is our mother, Christ, who would take on vulnerability, limping in the face of the Enemy, feigning her wing broken, wilting to sacrifice herself for her chicks, if need be."

I looked to my side to watch James. He was languidly chewing a blade of quack grass and watching the mama killdeer, this bird in his eyes an early summer incarnation of what it must mean to love somebody to death. That may be all we ache for in the end—to know that we are loved to death. One day I trust he'll understand that he is and always has been.

— 14 —

June 24, Midsummer's Day and John the Baptist's Day

The Word in Redi-Mix

> In those days came John the Baptist, preaching in the wilderness of Judea, "Repent, for the kingdom of God is at hand." . . . Now John wore a garment of camel's hair; and a leather girdle around his waist, and his food was locusts and wild honey.
>
> —Matthew 3:1, 4

Summer's sudden warmth brings things out. Like any warming, it sometimes brings things out that have lain dormant, stilled by cold or covered by cool discretion, things blanketed by the prevailing rules of privacy that often hide life. People in little towns do talk, of course, tirelessly and with sweet relish, about each other. And the more curious their neighbor's doings, the more talk there is. But for all the gossip, folks in small places give each other a wide berth. When conversation drifts to the especially enigmatic behavior of a neighbor or the obvious oddity of some shoestring cousin, it nearly always ends with a shrug of the shoulders, a stretch of reflective silence, and a ritual muttering of "each to his own," or "it's a free country."

In time people stop talking about even the strangest

behavior, partly because the exception is no longer exception if it persists long enough, and partly because after decades of gossip about the same people, there's finally little left to say. For example, no one has much discussed Ivar Johanson for decades. Most everything that might be said about Ivar had long ago been said through smirks and guffaws over beer at the Blue Spruce. Everything else had been said through sighs of compassionate resignation at every church coffee hour in town. It is indeed a free country, after all. Each to his own. And so it would have continued to be, each to his own in a free country, had it not been for a wet spring and the sudden heat of summer.

Ivar is a bachelor of indeterminate age, seventy at least, probably older. No one is quite sure. Though a bachelor who lives on a farm, a shy quarter-section of poorly drained land along the river nine miles west of town, he is not a bachelor farmer. He keeps a vegetable garden for himself: tomatoes and green peppers, neat rows of peas and potatoes, but he leases out most of his land dry enough to grow anything on to one of the Sodergren boys. He uses the money from the lease—not much, but enough—to buy what he needs: the food he doesn't grow himself, and every spring a fresh pair of bib overalls and a new pair of Red Wing work boots. But most of the money from the lease goes to buy bags and bags of Redi-Mix cement and rolls and rolls of chicken wire.

What Ivar has been doing with all that Redi-Mix and chicken wire had been a topic of wide speculation for two decades. The flow of Red-Mix gossip ceased only when every imaginable possibility had been exhausted. A swimming pool? A new foundation for the house? A bomb shelter? It would never occur to anybody to be so boldly rude as drive over there and poke around. Such an investigative visit would trespass local strictures about privacy. But people do ask Ivar once and again when he's in town. "Whacha makin' out there with all that Redi-Mix?" they inquire in jocular tones that hardly hide the intensity of their curiosity. His reply is always prefaced with a steely, unblinking stare and a disconcerting pause while he looks at the back of his questioner's eyeballs. Then he says, "Soon, you see pretty soon now."

Ivar doesn't own a car or a truck. His occasional forays into town are made astride an ancient Schwinn bicycle with white-wall balloon tires and red-and-yellow streamers attached to the ends of the hand grips. A builders' supply place in Mankato delivers the Redi-Mix, the fine grade made with sand rather than gravel, every couple of months. So it would still be if it were not for a particularly wet spring and summer's sudden heat.

The third week of June, Ivar rode the Schwinn into town and directly to the offices of Dr. Brian Wilson, our two-day-a-week family practitioner. The other five days of the week he doctors over in New Ulm. Ardis Wilcox works part-time as his receptionist and has let it be known that Ivar's answer to question number three on the Patient Visit Form that he filled out in the waiting room, the question that asked, "Last visit to a physician?," was "NEVER." She said he lettered it in capitals and underlined twice. The reason for this first visit ever, the answer to question four on the same form, Ardis said, was "swelling." Ivar did not write "swelling" in caps, nor did he underline it. But, Ardis says under her breath, "He really should have and he should have written it in red ink too."

Ardis told more than a few folks in town, including her husband, Larry, who told me. Old Ivar Johanson, the story had it, was a swollen mess from his ankles to his neck, a mass of bug bites, blackflies and mosquitoes both. Their seasons often intersect in June, their numbers and aggressiveness nourished by the wet of late May and the heat of June. Come that week, Ivar Johanson's damp riverside farmstead was doubtless alive with little things that bite. Doc Wilson was ready to put him in the hospital, but Ivar, the tale goes, negotiated hospitalization down to a shot of cortisone and a promise to come back in a couple of days if he was still swelling up. What intrigued the doctor, Larry told me, was the fact that the bites were everywhere.

"I mean everywhere," Doc Wilson said when he phoned me that same afternoon. He had made two calls after Ivar left the clinic that day, one to a county social worker and the other to the Lutheran church, guessing correctly that anybody named "Johanson" was bound to be a Lutheran. But the Lutheran pastor was up in Detroit Lakes on vacation for a few weeks. And when he's gone, the Lutherans are blessed with Presbyterian pastoral care. When I'm gone in late July and early

August, the Presbyterians are ministered to by the Lutherans. And we both cover for the Methodists who cancel church in the summer. Their ministers come and go so fast that they've never quite locked into the summer vacation rotation.

"I mean," Dr. Brian went on (he wants us to call him Dr. Brian), "he had bug bites everywhere, Reverend. There's only one way to explain those bites. There's no way he's wearing any clothes out there by the river."

I drove out to the farm two days later. The farmhouse is set well off the road, near the river at the end of a two-rut road kept open, one would assume, only by the regular visits of the truck that delivers the Redi-Mix. I knocked on the screen door of the small frame house set comfortably in a stand of old cottonwoods. Most of the paint was weathered off the clapboard. The house appeared almost camouflaged in its setting. The tall grass in the yard had been recently cut rough with a scythe. There were no foundation plantings, only a large and well-tended vegetable garden in front of the barn. There was no answer at the door. I knocked again. Still no answer. I returned to the car, only too ready to forgo a visit that was not really my worry and now set me a little on edge. I started the engine, but then mumbled to myself, "He's got to be here somewhere." I gave the horn two taps. Two sharp mechanical bleats from a '93 Taurus pierced the quiet of the cottonwood grove.

Ivar appeared from behind the barn and walked slowly toward the car. I noticed his hands first; they were covered with what could only be concrete. With one hand he was pointing. At first I thought he was pointing at me, but as he got closer it was clear that he was pointing his long, bony, concrete-covered finger at the hood of the Taurus. He wore not a stitch of clothing. His lean old body was already tanned, burned bark-red everywhere. And it was covered with a pox of whitish-gray specks of what could only be Redi-Mix concrete.

Pointing at the hood of the car, the engine idling, he called out, "'Da eart iss da Lord's and da fullness dereof.' Ain't you never heard of global warming, son? Turn dat damn machine off and leave it off." He turned and walked back toward the river beyond the barn. I turned the engine off, got out of the car, and followed him into the cottonwoods.

"Ivar," I called after him, "Doctor Brian is worried about you. People are worried. You okay?"

"Nefer better," he called over his shoulder without turning to look at me. "I'm almost done."

"Done with what?" I yelled after him.

We were into the cool of the cottonwood grove, descending toward the river. I could see a clearing beyond. "You're some kinds preacher, ain't ya?" he asked.

"Yah, Second Presbyterian in North Haven." I launched into an explanation of my visit, his obviously Lutheran name, the new Lutheran minister on vacation. He could not have been less interested.

"You're a preacher. Guess you can have a look den."

The grove opened into a grassy clearing, maybe a hundred yards across. The river was just beyond it, twenty feet farther down a steep bank. The meadow was high enough that it would never flood. As we emerged from the deep shade of the cottonwoods, the clearing was suddenly intensely bright and, for midmorning, surprisingly hot. Ivar didn't look at me for a reaction to what was in the clearing. Rather, he looked away, toward the water. The clearing, nearly round in shape, was circled by perhaps a hundred statues, some single figures, more of them in clusters of human and animal figures, all of them larger than life-size, all of them the white-gray of dried concrete. The entire scene was surreal and disorientingly out of place.

"Geez, Ivar . . ." I said, and then was lost for words. He was still uninterested in my reaction to his work. He had scrambled down the riverbank and was standing knee deep in the water washing the drying cement off his skin.

I spent the next hour circling the meadow and its huge ring of Redi-Mix art. The statues showed as much detail as modeled concrete would allow. Ivar was clearly a master of his bizarre medium. The figures were out of proportion in the way El Greco paintings are. They were invariably posed dramatically, even melodramatically, assuming demonstrative gestures: the back of the hand on the forehead in the manner of ladies swooning in Victorian pictures, fingers pointing so accusingly as to arch upward in much the way Ivar had pointed at the polluting V-6 under the hood of my Taurus. Brows were furrowed deeper than any mortal brow could furrow.

Many of his concrete figures were presentations of biblical scenes, invariably biblical scenes involving judgment. The first one, just to the left as you came down the path into the clearing, was of God (his size and the beard gave Him away) with Adam and Eve. An unnaturally long divine finger pointed up the hill back toward the farmhouse. Our first parents, crouching before Godly wrath, were portrayed slinking away from the river and up the hill toward Ivar's vegetable garden. This statue was obviously older than the others. It had already been much patched and repaired. At the bottom of each statue on massive Redi-Mix bases, bottle caps had been set in the concrete in such a way as to spell out captions. In metal dots that still said "Hires Root Beer" and "Hamm's Beer," this first read: "Adam and Eve are driven out of the garden to till the earth."

Ivar's biblical statues much favored the prophets: Elijah, brow furrowed at the dancing prophets of Baal, Nathan pointing his finger at King David. "Thou ART the man," read the bottle-cap caption. Jeremiah was there with his plumb line, five feet of green twine with a bunch of rusty washers tied to the bottom end. It hung straight from his outstretched hand, again reckoning the uprightness of all who passed by. Three tableaus were given over to the career of John the Baptist. Jesus' several parables of judgment were also well represented. The concrete presentation of the judgment between the sheep and the goats from Matthew 25 was necessarily elaborate. Its caption read, "Truly, as you did it to one of the least of these, you did it to me."

But interspersed among the biblical scenes as naturally as the clearing sat in the cottonwoods, there were also cement representations of current events, some more current than others, all from the sweep of the last forty years. Early in the circle there was a much repaired symbolic scene that obviously represented the cold war, a bearded deity pointing one arched finger at an American eagle and the other at a hammer and sickle, each of which was surrounded by Redi-Mix missiles slanted at each other. There were representations of the assassinations of Kennedy and King. Between them sat a hunched figure, face buried in his hands. Another complex set of figures represented the Vietnam War. Three-quarters of the way around the circle there was what looked like a police line-up of Redi-Mix presidents, Republicans and Democrats alike, their sins spelled out tersely in bottle caps at their feet, their heads bowed to divine judgment. Cast in fresher concrete was a representation of a mammoth television set, its oversized screen covered in bottlecap *X*'s and *R*'s. It was about to be smashed by a furious bearded figure with an old single-bitted ax set in his raised concrete hands: God killing your TV for you.

It was hard for me to make out the statue that Ivar had been working on when I arrived. It was unfinished, the cement was still green, there was no bottle cap caption yet. It was going to be large, perhaps five times the size of any of the others. It was architectural, with symmetrical rows of Greek columns, and populated with bowing angels and fiercer creatures in recline. Ivar had emerged from the river and was standing looking at his most recent—and from its place nearest the river in the circle—perhaps final work.

"Da heafenly city," he said looking away from the statue to the river, "da way tings oughta be. When I'm done," he went on looking at me for the first time since prophesying against my Taurus, "when I'm done, people can come and see. Dey can come for free. No charge. You announce it in your church."

Ivar had just finished that last statue, which he captioned "New Jerusalem," when he received the second visitor occasioned by Dr. Brian's concern. That visit went less happily than mine. It was made by a middle-aged social worker from the Mankato office who was less than taken with the rustic enchantments of rural life. She took a first look at Ivar's house without running water, a second at Ivar's outhouse (a convenience she had heard of but never seen), and, lastly, she took a third look—direct and frontal—at Ivar's concrete-bespeckled and bug-bitten nudity.

Still, nothing might have come of her visit. But after finding Ivar in the meadow, and after finding her tongue again, she mumbled disparagingly about the judgmental and righteous tone of his statuary. Ivar approached her in his unashamed altogether, took her chin, which she had only just dropped, and said, "You got good color lady, good bones, no reason to cover it up wit paint." With that he took the rag he had just used to clean himself in the river and wiped the lipstick and rouge from her flabbergasted face.

That act, labeled "assault" in the legal papers filed that next week, plus condemnation of the farm for non-payment of taxes and a list of code violations encyclopedic in its length, led Ivar to forced relocation in the Brook View Care Facility on Highway 14 just this side of Sleepy Eye. He went off happily enough last Monday afternoon after being told that he could indeed see the creek from his window. I wanted to be there, having been perhaps the first to ever see the man's life work. I watched as he climbed in the car for his first-ever automobile ride. He looked toward the river and the statues in the meadow and muttered, "Well, dat's done." The farm is up for sale. Rumor has it that Lyle Sodergren is interested, but can't get Ivar to negotiate.

I didn't have to announce anything in church, of course. Everybody from here to the Twin Cities knows about Ivar Johanson's statues by the river. Some art critic from Minneapolis has already named them "a classic manifestation of Midwestern folk art." There's talk of a township park and a fence to keep the kids out. Recently we got a visit from the Kohler Foundation over in Wisconsin. They specialize in preservation of the work of "untrained artists." They said that the statues could never be moved, but there might be a grant for the fence in the offing, maybe even enough money for an interpretation center and brochures to give people when they came to visit.

And people really do go out to the river to see what Ivar made, just as he hoped they would. They go out of curiosity, an early evening's outing to see what's out there. It beats sitting around and watching reruns of *Wheel of Fortune.* But when they drive home, so several have mentioned, it's always oddly quiet in the car. No one, it seems, ever has much to say after spending an hour with Ivar's statues by the river. Prophets—ones with words and ones without—are after all only prophets if they discomfort us, even strike us dumb, at least for the ride home or the walk back to Jerusalem.

— 15 —

July 7

Ultima Thule

> He charged them to take nothing for their journey except a staff; no bread, no bag, no money in their belts, but to wear sandals, and not to put on two tunics.
>
> —Mark 6:8-9

Never underestimate the danger hidden in the pages of books. Lamont Wilcox read books, every one of C. S. Forester's Horatio Hornblower novels, those epic sea adventures set in the Napoleonic Wars, and retreated to the barn to build a boat. He drank too much, neglected the farm, and finally sailed off to the Caribbean without his wife, Annette, who didn't want to go anyway. All this because his high-school English teacher, the late

Miss Pratt, had given him her old Book-of-the-Month-Club copy of *Captain Hornblower in the Caribbean.*

My daughter, Jennifer, who just graduated from high school this past month, also reads books, and what she read in her books got her, and her father, into trouble of sorts. Of all things, she took to reading the classics—in translation of course—as well as popular histories of the Greeks and the Romans. The ancients have fascinated her ever since a sixth-grade field trip to the University of Minnesota Museum, where she beheld what she soberly described to her mother and me upon her return that night as "very, very old things." In all the reading that followed, she stumbled across a mysterious phrase, half Latin, half Greek, that has puzzled scholars for centuries. These two words came to fascinate my daughter.

The ancients, she learned, believed in a place named "ultima Thule." They believed it existed and wrote of it, though they were not of one mind about precisely where ultima Thule might be. They were in agreement on only one point, that ultima Thule was the northernmost land of human habitation. Some historians have guessed it to be Norway, others the Shetland Islands or perhaps even Iceland. Wherever it lay, a spiritual mist enshrouded the very words. Ultima Thule was the end of the earth, the last place one could go, the ultimate destination. These last years, my daughter has discovered boys, the relationship between grades and getting into college, the inspirational tedium of working in the A & W Drive-In in New Ulm, and the anxiety provoked by letters arriving from the colleges to which she applied. Through all of these adolescent vagaries, ultima Thule has stood, it now seems, for a sanctuary in her adolescent soul, the place apart, the great destination, the journey's end.

Her daily bus rides to high school in Sleepy Eye that began four years ago have been a repeated harbinger for her mother and me, and I think for Jennifer herself, of her growing up and leaving us. Each day's journey to Sleepy Eye carried her closer to the day she would leave home for good. This is a prospect that every parent of a teenager greets with wildly mixed emotions. Annie said this spring that the only thing worse than Jennifer leaving home in the fall would be Jennifer staying home in the fall. When those bus rides began and continued into that first freshman winter, the big orange thing rumbling away in the dark of the morning and then the brakes squeaking to announce her return in the dark of the late afternoon, my daughter and I made an emotional lunge for each other, knowing the real parting that was coming in four short years. We were not ready for it then in the way we are now, and we made a rash promise. We promised each other that after high school, father and daughter would take a trip together, a very special trip.

The making of that promise fell on the dark early December morning of an impending snowstorm. The buses were running anyway. We were at breakfast; I was playing with my oatmeal and casting glances out the window every thirty seconds to look for snow and then back at my daughter, growing up too fast, fearless of the slippery roads between North Haven and Sleepy Eye. I was suddenly aware that everything was on the cusp of changing forever.

"When you graduate, Sweets, let's take a trip, just you and me, a father and daughter trip."

"Could we, I mean, really?" she asked.

"You betcha," I answered, relieved at her enthusiasm. "Where should we go?"

Her answer was unreflective and immediate: "Let's go to ultima Thule."

I remember looking at my oatmeal, then out the window to see the first snowflakes in the morning darkness, and saying, "Well, sure." Daughters have this way with fathers, my wife says. Anyway, it was four years off, and nobody knows where ultima Thule is.

The great trip was lost in the litter of high school, forgotten, or so I thought, until the day the acceptance letter came from Carroll College. She opened it after she got home from band practice late one April afternoon. After a squeal of joy at her acceptance, she noted that it said that freshman were to report for orientation on Wednesday, the 28th of August.

Jennifer read the letter aloud to us, accented that date, looked thoughtfully at me and said, "Dad, that means the trip will have to be in early July. That's the only time Doris will let me off from the A & W."

With that she left the room to start phoning friends. Annie looked at me and asked, "What trip?"

"The trip to ultima Thule," I said.

"Where?" my wife asked.

High school seniors, for all their fresh wisdom, have only the loosest grip on geographic and financial realities. When, on a Saturday morning in May, I outlined to my daughter the tuition, room, and board costs at Carroll, and then estimated costs of getting to even the most accessible of the possible locations of ultima Thule, she looked at the numbers on the paper in the same way that I might look at the Pentagon budget: the numerical imagination of mortals can scarcely ascend to such heights. Frankly I had thought that both ultima Thule and a trip with her father would have shed some of the intrigue they had held when she was four years younger, but not so. As she talked that morning, I came to understand that ultima Thule had become a necessary punctuation mark for my daughter in her passage from childhood to adulthood. It was a point of passage marked in ink on the map that she had plotted for her young life. But as her spirit matured in the years since she first asked to go there, ultima Thule had become something more. It was no mere spot on a map, but this furthest place was also the point of greatest spiritual inaccessibility, that deep and far place where hidden things might be seen.

So I took the map I had in my back pocket, not a map of the world, not a map of the United States, but a map of Minnesota. I unfolded it between us on the kitchen table next to the yellow notepad on which I had noted tuition figures and the estimated airfare for two to Norway. I smoothed its folds and pointed to North

Haven near the bottom. Then I pulled my finger slowly toward me, north, north past Willmar, past Sauk Centre, past Park Rapids and Bemidji, north across the two Red Lakes, north to the Lake of the Woods, and finally across that huge lake to a little nook of land surrounded by the water and attached only to Manitoba.

"The Northwest Angle," I said, "the ultima Thule of Minnesota. The only ultima Thule your old man can afford."

Minnesota's Northwest Angle is maybe the most notorious error in the history of modern surveying. The border between the eastern half of the U.S. and Canada is formed mostly by water: the St. Lawrence River, then four of the Great Lakes, and finally, between northeastern Minnesota and Ontario, by the Pigeon and the Rainy Rivers. The Rainy flows west into the Lake of the Woods, and there the border jogs oddly northward across that cold expanse of water to the point where it was supposed to meet the U.S.-Canadian border coming from the west, that twelve-hundred-mile line drawn straight with a ruler east from the Pacific Ocean. But somebody made a mistake, a twenty-five-mile mistake; the two borders didn't meet. They stranded a little hunk of Minnesota in the Lake of the Woods, a hundred square miles of land surrounded on three sides by lake, a nook of land and water jutting north above the international border like the valve sticking out of the top of an old pressure cooker.

Such a tale of historical accident and the obvious remoteness of the place made it an ultima Thule nearly as satisfactory to an eighteen-year-old as the Shetland Islands, but one that you could drive to. When I called for a cabin at a place called Angle Inlet where the road ends (and the only place in the Angle with a name), I learned that it was just twenty-some years ago that they built the road in from the rest of the United States.

"Used to be you had to get Faye to bring ya over from Warroad in his diesel boat," said Arne as he took my reservation. I was late to be calling, he said. The cabin was probably the last one available anytime in July anywhere in the Angle. And I could only get it for three days in the middle of the week. Long enough, I thought, to be in ultima Thule.

That my eighteen-year-old deigned to take a road trip with her father was a wonder to all who heard of it. But children, for all of their rumored spontaneity, are also lovers of routine and predictability. This trip had been a landmark in Jennifer's mental landscape for all the years I had forgotten I had made the offer. Her anticipation made her a garrulous traveling companion. We left right on a cool and bright Sunday afternoon just after church, skipping Annie's offer of lunch, eager to be on the way to ultima Thule. In the space of fifty miles, the front seat of the Taurus became something of a confessional booth. Away from the strictures of familiarity, Jennifer talked and talked, inspired to transparency (as we all often are) by the increasing proximity of what one has so eagerly awaited. Jennifer talked about her friends, about college, what she would major in, what her roommate from Milwaukee might be like. And for my benefit, I would guess, she allowed as to how she would miss her family, “but I’ll be home a lot of weekends, you know.” As she said the words, I recalled making that same hollow promise in equal earnestness a mere thirty years ago.

The drive is two-lane highway all the way; Minnesota 71 due north most of it. The miles and the words rolled on as open farmland yielded to stands of birch and pine, and then those occasional forests grew together into the “big woods” that stretch north to Hudson Bay. We stopped for the night in Bemidji. After dinner I took Jennifer’s picture with the awful statue of Paul Bunyan that you see on all the postcards. She’s a tall girl, but she looked tiny next to Paul. The next morning found Jennifer, and even her father, as full of expectation as a seven-year-old on Christmas Eve. Jennifer drove, too fast as I kept telling her. We had chosen an unlikely route, the road that skirts the west shore of Red Lake. The woods that flashed by on either side of the car were now unbroken, dark and impenetrable to the eye on that cool and overcast Monday. Not far beyond Warroad you cross the border into Manitoba. The blacktop gives way to gravel, mile upon mile of gravel slicing through the woods of Manitoba, and then we came to the sign proclaiming that long ago surveyor’s mistake: WELCOME TO THE UNITED STATES OF AMERICA.

We arrived in Angle Inlet exhausted. It had grown so cold that I had turned the heater dial on the Taurus well into the red zone. As Arne showed us to our cabin, it began to rain. He cast us a sideways glance and said,

"Hope it don't turn to snow." The cabin was small, illuminated by two once-modern fixtures hanging from bare wires, clearly design fancies of the sixties. Arne pointed at the fireplace and said kindling and firewood were out back. "Was there anything else you needed?"

The kindling, the firewood, and the newspaper were damp; everything was damp. Starting a fire descended into a comedy of errors. The heavy, wet air in the fireplace was loath to draw, the damp kindling smoked. Jennifer and I were in hooded sweatshirts pulled tight around our faces, both of us kneeling before the fire and blowing on the reluctant flames. We blew until I started to feel light-headed and she started to giggle. Then we laughed, laughed at us, laughed at this cold and damp ultima Thule, laughed until the fire smoked and went out. We ate Fritos and bean dip, put on all our clothes, found our sleeping bags, and went to bed, me on the couch in front of the fire that wasn't and Jennifer in the only bed.

I awoke with the sleeping bag pulled around my ears, but cold nevertheless. I looked into that first moment of wakefulness to see my daughter sitting at the table still in her sleeping bag. She was drinking Diet Coke from a can and had a map spread out before her. She was crying. I crawled out of the warmth into the very cold air of the cabin. On this July morning, the temperature in ultima Thule had fallen to the upper thirties.

I sat down across from her. "Disappointed?" I asked.

She nodded and dried her face with the sleeve of her new Carroll College sweatshirt. "I went for a walk just now," she said. "It looks like all the other woods we drove through. And it's cold. Arne says the only reason people come here is to fish. I hate to fish."

"You want to go home?" I asked.

I glanced at the map between us on the table. She shook her head and composed herself, looking at me as she does whenever she is getting ready to say something that she has been thinking about.

"Dad, it's not the being here, you know. It's the going. I mean, the best part of this whole trip was thinking about it all through high school. The drive was just as good, and stopping to see Paul Bunyan. Maybe the best part was trying to start the fire last night and blowing on the kindling together and the smoke in the cabin, and then laughing." She took a sip from her Coke can. "I felt like that when I graduated last month. Graduation wasn't much; it was the getting there. Next month I move to Wisconsin for college, and then I'll graduate in four years, and then I'll probably go to work or something. Who knows, maybe I'll get married and have kids. But none of those things are ever it; none of them are, like, the end. You don't ever arrive, Dad. It's the getting there, it's the trip itself that's the thing. There is no ultima Thule."

"So you ready to head home?" I asked.

She looked down at the map, which was, I noticed for the first time, not a map of Minnesota. It was a map of Manitoba. She pointed to a spot over on my side of the table, north, far north, the place where the roads ended and the tundra began.

"How long would it take us to get to Flin Flon?" she asked.

"Days," I said, "days of driving."

"Good," she said. "Let's go."

As we drove north through Manitoba, we talked, but not as much. I had decided to tell her our news on the way back from ultima Thule, the news that two months after she left for college, the rest of her family would also be leaving North Haven, the only home she knew. Annie had volunteered to talk to Christopher while we were gone. I had promised to talk to my daughter while we were on the road. But it was the right time, Jen off to college, Chris starting high school, and North Haven withering too small to either support or need the ministrations of three Protestant clergy—a Presbyterian, a Methodist, and a Lutheran.

At the special session meeting next Sunday after church, I would suggest that Second Presbyterian and Aldersgate United Methodist either share a pastor or start making plans to merge. I would do this right after asking them to call a meeting of the congregation so that they might vote to concur with my resignation. The suggestion about the Methodists would be greeted with sadness and relief. Both congregations have long understood that they have been inching inevitably toward some such compromise with reality. There would be some ironic historical symmetry to either course with the Methodists. When the old First Presbyterian had fought one of those tragically earnest doctrinal battles a hundred years ago, half the congregation left to form Second Presbyterian. And then, when First Church's building burned to the ground a few years later, the remaining stalwarts refused—on Presbyterian principle—to join Second Presbyterian and became Methodists instead. Now the mysteries of providence might yet bring their grandchildren to the same coffee hour.

Two weeks ago, Annie and I had flown into Detroit Metro, a grim bus terminal for airplanes where we had been picked up by Walt Ungerer, chair of the Pastor Nominating Committee of Westminster Presbyterian Church of Elm Forest, Michigan. They put us up for the weekend at the Dearborn Inn, Henry Ford's Great Depression vision of what an old American inn ought to look like. It was a welcome and winsome indulgence. Saturday, we had breakfast with the committee, a buffet of scrambled eggs, overcooked bacon, sticky sweet rolls, and then words that advanced from stilted and careful to fulsome and candid.

At eleven o'clock, Annie was whisked away by a local realtor for drive-by viewings (it was judged premature to actually go inside any houses) while the committee and I settled in for an interview in the church parlor. It went well, or so it seemed to me, as did the sermon I preached the next morning in the requisite "neutral pulpit." Neutral means not theirs and not mine, in this case the pulpit of First Presbyterian of Ypsilanti. They discreetly chose not to sit in one conspicuous lump in the half-full church. I preached the text for the day, a sermon I had preached three years ago on the same passage. Brunch with the committee at the Dearborn Inn after the service was warm, then jocular, marked here and there with flashes of intimacy.

On the flight home, Annie and I said little. We both sensed it had gone well. It felt perhaps like a call. When Walt phoned late Monday evening, Christopher answered the phone. Putting his hand over the mouthpiece as I walked toward him, he whispered suspiciously, "It's some guy from Michigan. What's up?" Annie and my trip to Michigan had doubtless sown seeds of suspicion in the minds of both kids, but they had asked no questions for fear of the answer.

We mulled it over for three days and called back on Thursday to say that we would come to Elm Forest. Ultima Thule it is not. It lies on the edge of what they name "Downriver," a cluster of look-alike suburbs that grew up after the Second World War and into the fifties and sixties, most of them thrown up fast to house the army of workers in the steel plants and automobile factories that lie to the west of the Detroit River and south of the city itself. Most of the houses looked like they might have emerged from the very assembly lines that employed the men and women they sheltered. But for their outward banality, this was a place that harbored a laudable loyalty. This fidelity and stubborn affection for place and neighbors were articulated time and again, both in and between the words of the nominating committee. They spoke of new libraries and hockey rinks, downtowns being spruced up, and three generations of family in the same neighborhood. Unlike North Haven, there were jobs, and the children did not always move far away.

All that was two weeks ago. I now watched Jennifer as she slept in the car, her head against the door resting on a pillow she had brought from home. She had slept at least half the miles we had covered on our way north to Flin Flon. I thought of her words over the map back in the cabin at Angle Inlet. They were somehow familiar wisdom. I knew I had heard or read something like them before. I remembered on the way home, just after I told Jennifer about the move. She cried but said she was not surprised. I told her that Detroit was closer to Carroll College than North Haven was. I did not mention that she would come home Christmases and summers to a place where she would know no one.

I finally remembered that it was Luther, of all people, who had said something like what Jen had said. I remembered just south of Wadena. I looked the quote up when I got home and typed it out and put the paper in an envelope, an envelope that Jennifer will find in the care package we would put together for the first month at college. What Luther said was this: "This life, therefore, is . . . not being, but becoming, not rest but exercise. We are not yet what we shall be, but we are growing toward it; the process is not yet finished, but is going on; this is not the end, but it is the road." Just so, Martin. There is no arriving in this life, no ultima Thule, only the blessed road.

— 16 —

September 14

Death to Flamingos

When the men of the town rose early in the morning, behold the altar of Baal was broken down, and the Asherah beside it. . . . And they said to one another, "Who has done this thing?"

—Judges 6:28, 29

The phone rang while I was drawing the shaver up my neck under my chin. Even with the water running it was loud enough to jolt my hand—a small nick.

"It's somebody from that Brook View nursing home place out on 14," Jennifer yelled up the stairs. "She says it's important."

I balanced my shaver on the edge of the old pedestal sink and went to the phone beside the bed, the sides of my face foamy and unshaven.

"Rev. Battles? This is Krista at the Brook View Adult Care Facility. We have a problem that we hope you might be able to help us out with. One of our residents, a Mr. Johanson, seems, well . . . seems to be . . . missing. He's a member of your congregation," she added in a tone that seemed to hint at culpability on my part, implying that I was a shepherd of wandering sheep. "We thought you should know. There's no family that anybody is aware of. We've just notified the county sheriff."

In truth, Ivar Johanson is a Lutheran, more or less. I got tangled up with him only because Arnie Norquist was on vacation. Arnie Norquist is the pastor of St. Peter's Lutheran in town. Forbiddingly pious though Ivar is, his church affiliation is an utter irrelevance to him. Suddenly it seemed less than essential to me. Even in the last corners of denominational tribalism, the old church lines drawn on the map of Europe half a millennium ago are blurring. So I did not bother to set Krista straight on Ivar's church affiliation, vague as it is. And the truth was, I wanted to know how the old man had managed to bust out of Brook View.

"When did you first miss him?" I asked in a bemused tone aimed to assign guilt to neither Brook View nor Krista, who sits, I knew from my visits, at the reception desk.

"Well, he was gone when the early shift came on, before I got here," she added with an edge of defensiveness. "The old fox stuffed a rolled-up blanket under the sheets to make it look like he was sleeping in his bed. He even swiped Mrs. Bjornson's wig. She's in 44. He stuffed it full with Kleenexes and put it on the pillow. They've both got about the same amount of white hair. The night shift, well, they never guessed. We figure he went out his window sometime after his bedtime which is, like, really early, about seven. Can you believe that, Reverend? He could be out there twelve, maybe thirteen hours by now. We never worried about anybody going out a window. They don't open that wide and most of our residents, well, they're just not that, you know . . . agile." She stifled what sounded like an amused giggle at Ivar's prowess at escape. "We thought he might call you up or something, what with those weird religious statues of his."

I promised that I would let her know if I heard anything. I wiped shaving cream off the mouthpiece of the phone, finished shaving, dressed, and called Larry Wilcox. Larry, as the town's other resident artist, has taken an interest in both Ivar and the old man's increasingly famous field of prophetic statuary. Ivar himself has no sense of being a member of any guild—artistic, religious, or otherwise. In fact, he would probably not think of himself as an artist at all. Larry thinks him one, however, and has taken to visiting Ivar in Brook View once and again. He does this out of a blend of unspoken charity and curiosity. The other day he mentioned to me that he brought the old man some black and white photos he had taken of the statues. Ivar had looked at them without hint of emotion and simply asked if people were coming to see them. When Larry said that they were, and "not only locals," Ivar had permitted something near a smile to crack his stony countenance.

"Larry," I said into the phone, "Ivar Johanson's busted out of Brook View. Seems he took off early last night. You know Ivar better than I do. Would you go out to his place with me? I betcha he just headed home. Can't say that I blame him."

I picked Larry up half an hour later, and we headed

west on 14 toward Ivar's farm. It lies north of the highway at the end of a long dirt road just this side of what's left of the town of Revelle. The entrance had once been marked with two rusted mailboxes, one at regulation height, the other (on which the words "air mail" were carefully lettered), on a piece of pipe about ten feet in the air. That whimsy, I thought to myself, surely must predate Ivar's tenure on the farm. Today we found the turn marked by a brand-new elaborately carved wooden sign, navy blue with gold-leaf lettering. It read, THE JOHANSON COLLECTION—VISITORS WELCOME. The Kohler Foundation had come through fast with a firm pledge of eighteen thousand dollars for preservation of the statues, some signage, a gravel parking lot, "visitors' interpretation center," and self-guided tour brochures. The county had gone ahead with the work, which was now nearly completed.

We parked the car and walked around to the rear of the house. The padlock had been pried off the hasp and the kitchen screen door stood open. We found a pair of Red Wing boots on the linoleum floor in the kitchen. They were caked with black mud that was just starting to dry to a dull silver-gray. In the small utility room off the kitchen, we discovered mud-splattered bib overalls and a red-plaid flannel shirt, both lying on the old Maytag wringer washer. Ivar wore flannel in all seasons, even the heat of August.

We went back into the kitchen. Hands on my hips, I looked out the screen door and into the cottonwood grove that surrounded the house. The uncut grass was overgrown, almost knee high. I turned to Larry, who was idly opening cupboards, looking for some hint of Ivar.

"I bet he's down at the river," I said. We left the house and headed down to the meadow where the curiously famous "Johanson Collection" stands in disarming glory—twenty-four cement prophesies, judgment spoken in concrete. It is consummately odd art, but as visitors have discovered to their surprise, oddly disarming as well. All summer, the statues have attracted an eclectic mixture of viewers: curious locals, folk-art buffs who find this more hard-edged art than they are accustomed to, and, of course, religious enthusiasts from the eagerly apocalyptic end of the theological spectrum. A recent article in the Mankato paper noted that these last visitors often find the political critique in the statues too uniformly merciless in their judgment of both left and right.

Ivar had been there, down by his river. At the center of his statuary circle, Kohler money had just erected a "Visitors' Center," an open, circular shelter twenty feet across. Under it, at the center, was a round metal interpretive map of the site. It was a four-foot wooden disc on top of which was a paper chart of the site covered with Plexiglas. Like a great compass rose, it was divided into twenty-four pie-shaped segments. In each section, words noted the location, name, and estimated date of execution of each of the works. It was nicely done and helpful in the same way that making biblical characters wear name tags would be. It would doubtless aid the visitor in keeping track of who is who, but would also surely organize some of the mystery out of the story. I remember Annie saying to me that stained glass looks different when you move it out of a church into a museum and put an informative label under it.

Fastened to one of the four-by-four pressure-treated pillars supporting the shelter's roof was a wooden box proffering the Kohler Foundation's newly printed brochures. Under the box was a sign: SELF-GUIDED TOUR BROCHURES—ONE PER VISITOR, PLEASE. I had first read the Self-Guided Tour Brochure a week ago and had set it down guessing that Ivar would not have much appreciated it. Larry had told me that after he had read it, he had decided not to bring a copy to Ivar. It had doubtless been authored by some summer intern at Kohler, couched as it was in the peculiar prose of art criticism, littered with subtly judgmental words like "untutored," "primitive," and "religiosity." One of these brochures was tucked under the hinged lid of the box, sticking out so that it would be seen. On its blank back, lettered large with a dull pencil, was a message: ONE MORE JOB—JOHANSON.

As we walked past the barn on the way back to the car, Larry noticed that the door was unlatched. He slid the reluctant hanging door open far enough for the two of us and the morning light to find our way in. It took a moment for our eyes to reconcile themselves to the dark of the barn, which smelled less sweet than most. Ivar had not kept animals, and there was no hay in the loft or on the floor.

"The old Schwinn is gone," Larry said, "and so's the trailer he built to pull behind it."

I remembered Ivar's forays into town for groceries—nine miles each way on a balloon-tired bicycle pulling a trailer. Larry turned around and looked into the corner behind us to our right near the door. A small wooden pallet lay on the dirt floor. He pointed at it and said, "There's a bunch of stuff gone. I know it was here; I saw it there two weeks ago. I asked Ivar if he wanted me to sell some of it off for him. He almost smiled, I remember. Then he said, 'Nope, might come in handy.' If I remember right, there were some hand tools. And there was an old Stihl chain saw and a couple of double-headed axes. And a nice acetylene torch with a small tank. David, you think somebody swiped the stuff?"

"Nope," I answered. "Ivar's up to something."

The morning was growing into as fine a day as ever September dreams. Warm it would be, but not too warm, cloudless and brilliantly lit. A wet July and August had finally quenched the thirst of a parched June. The green that had been hiding in the dirt had exploded at last, welcome, but too late for some farmers. As we headed east back into town, Larry was looking out the car window as the first of the nine miles rolled by. He'd said not a word since we had left the barn and was now staring intently out the car window. He was wearing a look somewhere between quizzical and reflective. I had guessed that he was seeing this familiar world with his photographer's eye.

I looked to see what he seemed to see and said, "It

really is pretty country. Nobody would come here to look at it, I mean, not like the North Shore. But it has its own kind of beauty. On a day like this you can see it."

I watched this slice of the undulating richness of southwestern Minnesota roll by, and I tried to look at it with attention and love. I strained to see through the veil of familiarity it wore. I knew I would miss it. Suddenly I recognized it more clearly than I had before. It manifested itself, the flat green fertility did; it appeared to me in the way a vision might, more pristine than I had remembered, clean and uncluttered, a layered landscape, unpretentious in its integrity. To the south I looked into a broad soybean field, intensely green. Between the road and the field, the ditch bloomed, an incidental garden of August wildflowers: a few purple lupine in the deep, wet stretches, Indian paintbrush, Queen Anne's lace, and yellow coneflowers up the drier sides. Beyond the bean field, an old windbreak of green ash trees waved their arms to the rising breeze like a pew full of Pentecostals at prayer.

"Stop the car!" Larry shouted without turning to look at me.

"What?" I answered.

"Pull over, David," he said softly as he smiled.

I pulled onto the gravel berm and had not even pushed the shift lever into park before Larry had opened his door and leapt out, leaving it hanging open. He stood looking east up Highway 14 toward North Haven, and then turned back west from the direction we had come. I was watching him over the roof of the car as he did this, and saw a smile of comprehension slowly spread across his face. He shook his head and chuckled. He looked at me and said, "You see what the old bastard has done?"

"What is it, Larry?" I asked. In reply, he raised his arm and swept it across the landscape to the south side of the highway. "Look at that," he said. I did, gazing down the road toward town, raising my hand to shelter my eyes from the morning sun, saluting the east. Then I turned to my right in a southerly arc and again recognized the loveliness of the land, wondering to myself why it had never shined through quite so clearly before.

"What do you mean? It's beautiful." I offered.

"Now turn around and look at the north side of the highway." Larry ordered.

I turned, leaned against the door frame of the car, and put my hands in my pockets, intent to pass his test. What I first noticed was a small billboard displaying a faded painting of a soft-serve ice-cream cone. The top of the curlicue was broken off. The words under it read, TRACY DAIRY CREME—SNACKS, BURGERS, COFFEE—10 MILES AHEAD. To the right was a speed limit sign, farther down the road was another, larger billboard, this one announcing an impending turn to reach one of the small resorts on Lake Shetak. "Left on 59!" it warned, the highway number followed by an insistent exclamation point. There was a stand of field corn on the other side of the ditch. In front of the field spaced at hundred yard intervals was that familiar parade of little seed company signs, each announcing the particular varietal planted behind them.

Then I turned back around to look over the car to the south side of the road. It was, I finally noticed, utterly bereft of signage—no billboards announcing the proximity of the Skelly Station in North Haven, no speed limit signs reminding drivers of the ubiquitous 55, no "Are You Saved?" interrogations, no seed company proclamations, nothing but soybeans, green and lush, the windrows beyond and wildflowers at our feet. Larry motioned for me to come around to his side of the car.

"You gotta see this," he said, edging his way down the near side of the ditch. I followed, and together we jumped the wet at the bottom and scrambled up the far side. As we reached the top, Larry stopped and pointed into the tall grass and flowers between us and the field. Up close, I saw what he had seen from the car—an old billboard, a rectangle maybe twenty feet by ten, lying face up and dead in the Indian paintbrush, staring up at the cloudless September sky. Together we looked down at it as you might a fallen enemy. NORTH HAVEN PIGGLY WIGGLY, it read, WHERE PRICE AND QUALITY MEAT. It had been felled with a chain saw, cut off low and neatly at the legs, as had a dozen others on the south side of the highway between Ivar's place and town. The metal road signs, for their part, had been brought down with the acetylene torch.

We were in town when we heard the siren, pulled up to our lone stop sign at the corner of Main Street and Adams. It was not the town's emergency warning siren we heard, dread voice heard every other year to warn of tornadoes. It was not the more familiar sound of the

EMS ambulance. It was not a police siren properly speaking, since North Haven had discontinued police service after Billy Hobart retired, but rather one of the county sheriff's cars crying out alarm. We looked at each other; Larry pointed his thumb down Adams Street. "It's close," he said, "a block or two down."

Any imaginative projection we might have made on the basis of what we knew to be missing—Ivar, his Schwinn with its trailer and probable contents—could never have prepared us for what we saw when we pulled up to the corner of Monroe Street. There were two Brown County sheriff's patrol cars, both with their lights flashing and sirens wailing. One was up on the lawn in front of the Gunderson's house at the corner. The other was moving down Monroe toward us at a pace just steady enough to keep abreast of Ivar, who was not in the street, but steadily progressing across the lawns between the sidewalk and the houses. Ivar was on his bicycle, handlebar streamers dancing, the trailer wobbling after him. The deputy in the moving car had just turned his siren off and his loudspeaker on.

As we pulled up behind the other patrol car, we heard an amplified voice of the deputy, young and pleading, "Sir, we are going to have to ask you to please bring your, uh . . . vehicle to a complete stop immediately. Sir, please. . . ."

The other deputy had parked his patrol car on the lawn where it might block Ivar from crossing Adams. His cap was pushed back and he was leaning on his open door. As I got out of the car, he had just reached down and unsnapped the top of his holster, his hand resting on revolver it held. I approached him quickly and introduced myself.

"Officer, I know the guy. He's harmless. Riding a bike on people's lawns, it's not exactly a capital offense."

"That's the least of it, Reverend. Look, there he goes again."

I turned to look down Monroe Street. Ivar was just about to pass through the MacDowells' front yard, bumping along at a respectable two-wheeled pace. He entered their lawn and veered to the right, closer to the house. He raised his arm, which I suddenly noticed held a double-bitted ax. He managed it with one hand, steering the Schwinn with the other. The ax swept back in a graceful arc and then rapidly down and forward. With one deadly stroke, he cut off Minnie's two plastic flamingo lawn ornaments at their one-quarter-inch dowel knees, hallow pink plastic imitations of birds never seen in this corner of the world, and not to my mind half so lovely as a wood duck. They flew for the first time in their fiberglass lives, landing gracelessly in the Schwinn's wake. Ivar saw us, but trained his resolute gaze not on the cop car in his more distant path, but rather on the little wooden Dutch boy and girl in his path, the pride of Bud Jennerson's wife, Alida.

Bud had heard the commotion and had just come out of his front screened door. He stood at the foot of his front steps, still in his bathrobe. He looked at the police cruiser now at the end of his driveway and then at Ivar

Johanson lumbering along on his ancient Schwinn. "Ivar, for God's sake . . . ," he called out stepping forward. Then he saw the ax and quickly decided not to die for the little wooden Dutch children and their windmill.

The word Ivar used repeatedly at the hearing in New Ulm was "cleansing." All prophets are either self-appointed or appointed by God, depending on your perspective on such things. There was no whisper of doubt in Ivar's mind on this question. He knew ugly when he saw it. He knew beauty when he saw it. And he knew in which direction God leaned in matters of both truth and beauty. Having spoken in concrete for God on the question of truth, he had turned his ax, chain saw, and torch to the matter of beauty. As it turned out, Ivar will not return to Brook View, but to a larger facility in Mankato, one better equipped to manage troublers of Israel. The incident has served only to increase interest in the "Johanson Collection," sure testimony to the truth that all publicity is good publicity.

Everybody in town admits that the cleansed south side of Highway 14 west of town looks much better than the uncleansed north side, which Ivar had planned to take care of on the way home. He had worked fast through the night and early morning, slaying twelve billboards, innumerable Minnesota Road Commission signs and seed company signs, not to mention seven flamingos, four gnomes, two Dutch boys, three Dutch girls in town, and one painted plywood fat lady bent over with her bloomers showing. He had deliberately spared only Elma Krepke's Virgin Mary in the upended bathtub—whether out of deference to her piety or the heft of cast iron, no one knows.

The road commission showed up in no time to replace their slain signage, much of it superfluous, some advising of unavoidable bumps and obvious turns in the road, others of the possible presence of deer. But most of the assorted commercial signs have not been raised again. In fact, half of the businesses they promoted are out of business. The question all this has raised around town is the question long asked about all prophets: What gives them the right? Who is Ivar Johanson to cut down private property, even if everybody is happy enough to see it gone? This, of course, has always been the problem with all the Ivars who have ever ranted and raved, chopped and torched, that long line of prophets, cranks, and futurists. Who are they to discomfort us? Larry had put our question well, "Even when they're right, what gives them the right?"

— 17 —

September 28

Coming and Going

For this corruptible must put on incorruption, and this mortal must put on immortality. . . .

—1 Corinthians 15:53

Minnie's wolf came for her in late September, the

Monday morning after an early frost, deep in Ordinary Time, that long stretch of days between Pentecost and Advent. It was a fit time perhaps, for death and birth seem the most ordinary things. Yet for their ubiquity, both are extraordinary. Both occasion reverence among us, even among the most irreverent. Birth and death are among the few things about which we are loathe to speak too casually. Both force whispers and invite considered words. Like the Hebrew name for God—all vowels, the sound of breathing—they are simply too holy to tack down with consonants.

Angus had read the Scripture lessons in church one Sunday in midsummer. Even at ninety-one, his voice is deep, if no longer strong. He reads with his mouth close into the microphone with a studied slowness, appearing to savor the taste of the words on his lips, underlining important verses by clearing his throat before them. He was well able to move to and from the lectern without help, though I involuntarily mouthed a prayer after he finished the reading and successfully descended the steps from the chancel back to his pew. He had held the ball-shaped knob on the corner old oaken chancel rail and took the steps right foot first, bringing his left down alongside the right before daring the next. Minnie was in church that Sunday, her last time in worship.

The Old Testament reading for the day had been from the lectionary's Jacob cycle, that collection of earthy Hebrew tales from the latter chapters of Genesis. Specifically, it fell to Angus to read Genesis 29:16-30. In a mere fifteen verses young Jacob, who is on the lam fleeing from the justified rage of his half-brother, Esau, falls in love with his lovely cousin Rachel and works seven years for her father to pay the bride price. The night of the wedding, this slippery father, who is also an uncle on his mother's side, pulls a bait-and-switch operation and stuffs his older daughter, Leah ("whose eyes were weak"), into the wedding dress and the marriage bed. Come morning, Jacob is furious, though in truth he has only gotten from his uncle what he gave his brother. This moral symmetry is lost on the young man, but he agrees to work another seven years for the hand of Rachel.

It strikes me as ironic that Bible publishers put indelicate material like this inside delicate white leatherette covers with fussy gold lettering. Often they install zippers on such Bible covers, zippers which appear too insubstantial to lock up bawdy tales like this, much less the God who seems to revel in them. Twice in the course of these fifteen verses, it fell to Angus to read before the entire congregation, his pastor, and his wife of nearly seventy years, the graphic Hebrew circumlocution "and he went into her," first with regard to Leah and then Rachel. Holy Scripture is much less delicate than most Christians are. If these words had not been in the Bible, Angus would have never spoken them. As it was, he had to veritably expel them out of his mouth. Knowing they were coming, each time he approached the words in the text he hesitated, swallowed hard, cleared his throat and spat them downward onto the page where they belonged, careful to look at neither me nor Minnie nor the congregation.

Angus cannot find comfortable words to speak of Minnie's death either. Hers was a death that had approached with more than one well-ordered rehearsal, but these preliminary run-throughs proved to be no more real than a play without an audience. Minnie had come home from Brook View last April with a sweet-spirited hospice worker at her side. Audrey was a farm girl from the other side of Marshall who had watched the barnyard routines of death and birth since she was a child. She had trained for the work in Minneapolis and had doubtless learned about the "stages of dying." This wisdom, however, she wisely spared Angus and the boys.

Angus said little in the course of my pastoral calls over the summer and into September. He would escort me wordlessly through their fussy parlor, past his La-Z-Boy, and up the stairs to their bedroom. Minnie and hospice had taken over the room, which betrayed some of the inevitable clinical ambiance of modern medicine. A mechanical hospital bed was pushed under the south window, ten feet from the old four-poster that they had shared for nearly three-quarters of the century. Angus was learning to sleep in it alone. There was no other machinery; Minnie had disallowed that, but there was a table neatly set with assorted medications. On the shelf underneath lay a stainless-steel bedpan atop the extra foam mattress pad, a precaution against bedsores.

My last visit fell two days before she died. She did not prompt me to ask her "the question." She knew the answer, and I knew she knew the answer. But I read the psalm, the twenty-third, and prayed the Lord's Prayer. Her lips moved as we prayed, silently forming the words. After the prayer we sat, held close by quiet. Then as I pulled my hand away, she raised hers. It was shaking, but as she touched my cheek it stilled. It was not her pastor she caressed, but her sons and her husband, perhaps the world. Her eyes held no fear. That prayer had been answered. The fear that had followed her home eighty-four years ago, watching with yellow eyes, pacing in the woods alongside the road toward her parents' farmhouse in Otter Tail County, had fled at last.

Larry had returned to North Haven over Labor Day weekend and stayed. This matter-of-fact manager from Spokane, entering middle age and no more loquacious than his father, had grown angel wings in these last weeks, so attentive a son was he. He made coffee and shopped, read the *Reader's Digest* aloud to Minnie, and played endless games of cribbage with his father. Such a wonder: the true test comes, and the least auspicious students rise to moral brilliance. Donnie came home just in time for the funeral and wept like a child, some tears for grief, of course, but more for regret.

The Sunday before that last call, our third child was baptized. It was I who baptized my own daughter, a new experience in life after all these years. The older two had been born before I was ordained to ministry. At first I had thought that I should be only a father that day, answering the parents' baptismal questions at my wife's side. It would have meant finding a spare minister, of course. But Annie persuaded me that she could well answer for the both of us, pointing out that the opportunity to baptize my own child would not come my way again. My own child's older siblings stood on either side of their mother, proud now, and taken with their new sister. At first Jennifer had been shocked that her parents had permitted such a thing to happen. Chris was at an age to be embarrassed by it, a pregnant mother being sure evidence of the very behavior narrated in the twenty-ninth chapter of Genesis in the bedroom next to his. But in the latter months of the pregnancy, our parental anticipation proved contagious. And each fell in love, even Chris so conscious of appearances, the moment they first held her. She had come three weeks early, an emergency Cesarean determined to enter the world feet first. I told Annie she just wanted to stick a toe out to see if she was ready for such a strange and risky place. She was small, barely five pounds, and did not come home from Lutheran Hospital in Mankato for a week.

The rephrased baptismal questions seemed awkward on my lips:

"Do we trust in Jesus Christ as our Lord and Savior?"

"We do," my wife answered for us.

"Do we promise to live the Christian faith and to teach that faith to our child?"

"We do," she answered again.

"Do we renounce evil and all that would defy the love and righteousness of God?"

"We renounce them."

A friend had told me once about a baptism he had witnessed on the island of Crete. It was held at dawn, he said, as was local custom, just as the sun rose. These preliminary questions were put to the family outside, just in front of the church. As they answered the last, the one about renouncing evil, all the family and godparents turned away from the rising sun to the west, still dark, and spat vigorously. They spat at the devil, brave souls.

Presbyterians don't spit in church, so Annie just handed me my daughter after answering the questions. I took her in my arms and arranged the train of her gown so that it fell nearly to the ground. I dipped my hand in the font and three times scooped warm water over my child's head, enough water so that it ran down her nose and back down the blond fuzz. She blinked, rolled her eyes upward in alarm, and screamed a thin, sharp cry. Just the right reaction to baptism. No cozy little ceremony this, but a passage through deep water, a little rising from death into life, a turning from dark to light. More than once I have been tempted to pinch placid infants who seemed too at ease with their baptisms.

Over her wails I called out, "Eleanor Grace, I baptize you in the name of the Father and of the Son and of the Holy Spirit."

Eleanor was after Annie's mother, whom we lost two years before, a venerable old-lady name not likely to make a comeback. Grace we added because she is a grace.

She was held and admired at coffee hour, doted upon

by her family of God. At least ten grandmothers drew their old wrinkles close to her young wrinkles and asked her, "Did your daddy make you cry?" She slept in reply. Angus and Minnie were not there, Minnie too weak for outings, Angus refusing to leave her alone. As we pulled out of the church lot, Annie looked into the backseat where Eleanor Grace, Child of the Covenant, slept in her car seat between her older brother and sister.

Then Annie had said, "Let's stop at the MacDowells on the way home."

Jennifer and Chris protested, so we dropped them off at home before making the visit. Surprise calls are still acceptable manners in this corner of the world. Larry looked a little bewildered when he answered the door, but Angus was on his heels pulling my coat off and offering coffee even before we had a chance to apologize for not calling ahead. Annie lifted the baby from her seat and carried her upstairs while the men turned their wits to coffee brewing in the kitchen. I asked no questions about Minnie. They only demanded words Angus did not have in him. Larry poured four coffees into Minnie's best china, old Wedgwood with gold Grecian figures circling both cup and saucer.

Then he said, "Take this up to your wife, Dad, and I'll stay down here for a minute."

Annie was laying the child into the old woman's eager arms as I stepped through the door. It had been a "good day," Audrey had noted in the hallway. She added that Mrs. MacDowell had been alert since midmorning. I stopped where I stood, balancing the cups on their saucers, watching and listening. Eleanor Grace was waking and starting to wail again. Minnie could not raise her arms more than a few inches from her body, so Annie was folding them around the child, still resplendent in her grandmother's flowing christening gown. "There, there," I heard Minnie whisper.

The baby stilled and Minnie looked into her eyes and said, "There's nothing to be afraid of." Then she looked away from the baby eyes into the eyes of her mother and said, "There really isn't."

As I looked down from the pulpit two weeks later into the first pew, I wondered if it is true that there is nothing to be afraid of. Angus stood for the hymn, tearless, the book resting on the top of the pew in front of him. He did not sing. He never did. He was flanked by his two sons. Down the pew were his daughter-in-law and three grandchildren, six-year-old Skip stroking the clip-on tie he had proudly demonstrated for me in the church parlor just before the funeral.

Is there really nothing to be afraid of? Have all the mothers who have cooed those words to their sleepless babes been telling lies? A disease marches deeper into your body for a decade and a half, refusing to take your life, leaving that to some lesser ally. For nearly seventy years two lives had woven themselves together, and with one pull, the warp is unraveled from the woof. An old man has to sleep alone in a double bed at the age of ninety-one, brewing tiny pots of coffee in the morning, pouring half a can of Campbell's cream of tomato soup into a saucepan and covering the rest with plastic wrap before putting it back in the frig, sliding a single TV dinner into the microwave, watching the clock over the television so that he does not start his dinner earlier than five o'clock. Is there nothing to be afraid of?

Angus had voiced no hymn preferences, so we were singing my choice, "A Mighty Fortress." The images are unapologetically martial: "For still our ancient foe doth seek to work us woe; His craft and power are great, And armed with cruel hate; On earth is not his equal." Minnie, it occurred to me, had not been afraid, but not precisely because there is nothing to be afraid of. There is so much to be afraid of. The truth—and I know she knew it—is more subtle. There is plenty to be afraid of, but in spite of it, you don't have to be afraid. "We will not fear . . ." we sang, "the prince of darkness grim, We tremble not for him, His rage we can endure, For lo! his doom is sure. One little word shall fell him."

I preached that little Word, for I have no other that might suffice. The first and the last word of the faith. To the shepherds the angels sang, "Do not be afraid." To the women at the tomb the angel said, "Do not be afraid." Do not be afraid, not because there is nothing fearsome. Do not be afraid because the fearsome things do not have the last word.

I told the story of Minnie's wolf; she had told me that I might. Not even Angus had heard of that eighty-year-old wolf. I told them how afraid she said she had been that afternoon when she was eleven. I told them about the scene that met her when she opened the door, her father with tear-swollen eyes, her silent mother, and incomprehending baby brother, her sister, Gertrude upstairs, the family's lone loss to the Spanish Influenza.

"I was first tempted to think that her wolf had caught up with her after all these years. She had dodged it for four generations, but now it had her. But no. Oh, it has chased her home again all these years later. But this time when she opened the door to the farmhouse in Otter Tail County, her father held out his arms, beaming. Gert had come downstairs and was standing at his side."

The Women's Association organized the reception in Fellowship Hall that followed the interment. A banquet it was, replete with heavenly manna: tuna-noodle casserole with potato chips crushed on top, chicken wings and blue cheese, Jell-O salad with baby marshmallows, Texas sheet cake, and urns of the best church coffee. The hall was arranged as it usually was for such occasions with rows of metal folding chairs back to back. I had offered Angus my condolences twice, the first time three days ago at the house as we waited for the undertakers, and then at the graveside just an hour ago. Each time, he had offered me his hand, held my gaze, and nodded stiffly. No words, but articulate enough if you knew the man.

Well into the reception, just as mere acquaintances were starting to leave, I found him sitting alone with James Corey. During the service, I had noticed James wedged between his mother and grandmother, a pew behind the MacDowells. He had wept silently through the service, an odd way for a child to cry, especially one so unafraid of his own voice. It struck me that he did not want Angus to hear him. He was, after all, weeping Angus's tears for him.

I had just left the child's mother and grandmother in conversation with Angus's boys, Larry and Donnie, both women proffering promises to clean the house and look in on their father after the boys had gone home. Promises I trusted they would keep, though it would not be enough. Angus had been left sitting with James. Even the most unflappable of comforters had found the old man's silence a frustration. James had sat down next to him, a giant slice of Texas sheet cake balanced in the palm of his hand. I sat on the other side of the old man and decided not to offer condolences again. Instead I dared to rest my hand on his far shoulder. He answered by not pulling away and looking at the linoleum.

James peered around the front of the old man and addressed me, "He's really sad, Dave. When he's really sad, he doesn't talk much." He took a bite of cake leaving globs of frosting at the corners of his mouth. Then this child who had wept the old man's tears spoke the old man's words. "It's like a monster came and cut his arm off. That's how he feels." Indeed, it must be like amputation. Such is the price we pay when we love deep and long. But the price of the alternative is unthinkable.

Yesterday afternoon I looked in on Angus. Larry and Donnie have returned to Washington State and California respectively. Larry, Angus told me, calls every other night. I can't quite imagine what their conversations consist of, once the liturgical "How you doing?" questions are answered with, "Fine, just fine." And following that, there is only so much to say about weather, gas mileage, and the Vikings.

The Monday after the funeral, Angus and I were sitting at the kitchen table talking football when James burst through the back door without knocking, dragging his backpack behind him. I watched Angus's face light up as he reached one arm out to the child who slid close to him, though still only half out of his jacket. He threw it on the floor and wiggled up onto the old man's knee, wrinkled his nose, and said, "Your breath stinks."

Angus smiled and answered, "You ready to watch them Munsters?"

— 18 —

November 3, All Saints' Day

Going and Coming

> From now on, therefore, we regard no one from a human point of view. . . .
>
> —2 Corinthians 5:16

James was at our front door early Halloween night, again this year in Donnie MacDowell's old ghost outfit. In one hand he held a plastic jack-o'-lantern already half full of booty: bite-size Snickers and Milky Ways,

Pez refills, and one despised apple. In the other he held Angus, a seed cap perched on his head, the bill unfashionably flat. James's eyes, I noted, were perfectly aligned with the holes in the bed sheet. He fairly screamed "Trick or Treat" at me as if it were one word. I slipped three Almond Joy singles into the jack-o'-lantern. He looked to see what the take was and then back up at me and asked, "Why do you have to go away?" I hedged, the answer being too long for the front steps. But the truth was that he didn't really want an answer. Like all children and most adults, he just didn't want anything to change. Hearing my words for what they were, he gave Angus's hand a tug and said, "C'mon, let's hit the Jennersons."

Most of the manse's contents that belong to us were already packed in the mountain of Mayflower boxes that filled the living room and two of the upstairs bedrooms, waiting to be swallowed by the moving truck that would come Monday morning. The house belonged to the church, as did much of the furniture. Clipboard in hand, the Mayflower man had noted almost apologetically that everything the Battles owned in the world would easily fit into "one of our little twenty-footers. That'll save the church out in Michigan a few bucks." Most of the contents of Jennifer's room had already left in late August aboard a U-Haul trailer. She and I had driven it to Wisconsin, just the two of us on the road again. Annie wept as she waved farewell to one daughter from the front stoop with another in her arms. I left trailer and daughter in Waukesha and drove back alone the next morning. At least, I said to myself again and again, she would be closer to us after we moved to Detroit. Chris was having a hard time of it, of course. North Haven is the only home he remembers, and no explanations of this move, however pressing, even crack the surface of his adolescent grief. Annie and I, for our part, are both an alchemist's brew of sorrow and anticipation.

Angus, James in tow, had stopped by four weeks ago on the Sunday afternoon of the day I announced to the congregation that I had accepted the call of the Westminster Presbyterian Church of Elm Forest, Michigan. I had then read the session's call for a congregational meeting "to concur with the request of the Rev. David Battles for the dissolution of the pastoral relationship between him and Second Presbyterian Church." They were not surprised; the surprise has always been that we stayed so long. They were accustomed to their pastors rolling over every three to five years, lured to larger places by the promise of people their own age and a living wage. As always, their response was a mixture of sadness, resignation, and anger. A colleague of mine had quipped at last month's presbytery meeting, "They'll be mad at you. They'd be mad even if you'd been there fifty years and they didn't like you." This time, however, the congregation's fruit punch of emotions was spiked with the dawning awareness that I would doubtless be the last pastor of Second Presbyterian Church. Some new thing, including Methodists it would seem, was rising with the irresistible buoyancy of necessity. They did not like it at all, though they liked the Methodist Rev. Melinda Ackermann. They liked her "even if," as Alvina Peterson put it, "she's one of those lady ministers."

As I had taken his coat, Angus said that he had stopped by "to talk," a prospect that caught my attention. The weight of years, the advent of James, and perhaps grief, have finally given the old man a few more words than he ever had. Nevertheless, "a talk" with Angus did not usually require you to take off your coat. We went in the kitchen and sat at the maple dinette—church property, I noted to myself. Angus cradled a coffee mug in his hands. It had a fading stencil of the church building on one side, and on the opposite side, the barely legible words: SECOND PRES—COME AS YOU ARE. It was a relic of one of my predecessor's several church promotion schemes. To my mind it invited the question, How else would you come?

"I just want to say thanks, that's all." Angus began, looking at the cup and not at me. "Thanks for staying. Thanks for being so good to Minnie. That's all."

It was something of a speech for Angus MacDowell, multiple sentences, no levity to deflect the gravity. And he did not ask me why I was leaving. I nodded appreciation; anything more would have only embarrassed him. But the truth was that "thank yous" were as awkward for me as for him. It was disconcerting to hear appreciation when I was haunted by the damning question of just what, after all, I had to show for ten years of ministry in this place. The church I had feigned to lead for a decade would surely soon have to merge if not close its doors. Everything measurable about Second Presbyterian was smaller: the church roll, weekly attendance, Sunday school, the budget. But, of course, I argued in my own defense, so was all of North Haven. Everything in town had withered if it had not entirely dried up and blown away. These recriminations were exacerbated at least three times a week when the stack of church junk mail on my desk would include three-color brochures advertising church growth seminars. Inside these missals were photos of pastors in business suits smiling over their testimonials to the recent dramatic growth of their respective flocks. At the center of one especially lavish brochure was a panoramic photo of the inside of a new church somewhere in suburban Tulsa, a semicircular auditorium that would easily hold the entire population of North Haven and the two surrounding counties. I could not but read judgment in their slick pages.

I said as much to Angus, the only soul save my wife to whom I had shriven myself on this matter. I told him how it gnawed at me that Second Church would doubtless have to edge its way into some generic Protestant alliance, a "North Haven United Community Church," or some such. He raised his eyebrows, looked at me, and said, "Humm, 'United Community Church'? Not too bad." He stroked the stubble on his chin, gray and irregular, for his shaving was becoming hit and miss.

"Take it from this old coot," he went on. "Don't you go and measure your life that way. Somebody will always be aheada ya. No need to keep track. It's all gonna be okay. We're gonna be okay. Took me the better part of a century to figure it out not to go and measure. Hope it don't take you so long."

This is the lesson I never learn. It is the raw Gospel, and you must keep learning it, but never quite learn it. Faithfulness is all that is needful, that one thing. And, if in the course of such faithfulness, success should rise in her steady wake—amen, so be it. And if in the same course of faithfulness, success does not rise in an equally steady wake—amen, so be it. I know this. I know that, directly pursued, success is the insatiable bitch goddess, luring her devotees deeper, always deeper, forever demanding more, just a little more. What was it Eliot had prayed? "Teach us to care, and not to care." I quoted Eliot to Angus, who was not impressed, but understood and nodded.

As he did so, James had stepped ever so gently into the kitchen, as if stalking a fawn on moccasin feet. In his arms he held Eleanor Grace, wrapped in a yellow crib blanket and sleeping. Annie was two steps behind him.

"Shhh," he whispered, "she's asleep, you guys."

Forgetting his whisper, James told us that he had never held a baby before, "Not even one." He sidled up to an empty chair at the table and, assisted by Annie, got himself onto it with the child still in his arms.

He looked into the child's face and said, "She's so tiny. Was I ever this little?"

"Not quite so small," I answered, recalling the only

time I had ever held James, the Christmas Sunday morning nearly seven years ago when he was baptized.

Some thought suddenly landed in the child's mind, illuminating his face. "She's a mini, that's what she is, a mini."

He laughed riotously; so did Angus covering his mouth, rousing "Mini" in no time. James returned the child, now wailing loudly, to her mother. Angus, having awakened the little mistress, made the noises that announce when it was time to go. He rose and strode over to the sink and set his coffee cup in it. Then he turned to me, looked at James, and said, "Well, I think its about time me and the little Success here wandered on down the street."

My last day in church was the first Sunday in November, the day we keep All Saints' Day, the third of November. We keep it in a Protestant way, declaring against evidence to the contrary that all of us are saints and holy to God and each other. I preached about All Saints' first, preached from the first verse of the fifth chapter of 2 Corinthians: "for we know that if the earthly tent we live in is destroyed, we have a building from God, a house not made with hands, but eternal and in the heavens."

Then I preached farewell, also from the same chapter, the sixteenth verse: *From now on, therefore, we regard no one from a human point of view.* I told them that they had done nothing to bring this move about and that I would miss them. I told them they were my patron saints, even the most intractable and foul tempered of them. Then I told them a story, something of a preacher's chestnut, retold time and again with permutations in detail, surely apocryphal and vaguely sentimental fiction, but true nevertheless.

"Somewhere in the Middle East," I began, "ages ago, there was a monastery with only a handful of monks. It was a tired old place, this monastery. Time and relentless labor, isolation, the hot sun, and the sameness of the days had ground the place down. Spirit had been drained from their life together.

"The abbot is the only one who really notices this slow erosion. He laments it, but is just too tired, too worn out to do much about it. God seems to have moved to the other end of the universe, leaving them alone to go through the motions. The abbot is also the one among them who most often leaves the monastery, usually to go to the nearby desert town to do errands. He happens to strike up the acquaintance of the rabbi of the town's synagogue, a community as dwindling and lifeless as the monastery. They are drawn together mostly by a common despair. The two friends spend hours together lamenting what used to be, mourning the poverty of spirit in both their places and their own lives.

"One day, as the abbot is headed into town, he meets his friend wobbling toward him, exhausted from trying to run the distance from the town to the monastery. He finds the rabbi animated, speechless, and gesturing madly, obviously bearing some urgent news. The abbot sits him down under a scrawny tree at the side of the road and tells him to relax. The rabbi first manages to communicate that he is losing his voice, and then that he has had a dream, a dream more vivid than any he has ever had—sharp and clear, an incontrovertible word from on high—and it has to do with the monastery.

"Again his voice leaves him, but his passion to tell his friend of his dreams will not be deterred. With a trembling hand, he grabs a sharp stone and scratches a few Hebrew words in the dry dirt in front of them. The abbot, also a scholar, reads the words and gasps in horror and incredulity. 'Are you sure?' he asks. The rabbi nods his head vigorously. The words in the sand read, 'The Messiah—among you.'

"The abbot shakes his head and laughs out loud, laughter edged with bitterness. 'The Messiah!' he says, 'one of my pathetic crew, not likely.' But the rabbi is fanatically insistent about the clarity of his dream. He presses upon his friend that what he has dreamt can be no other than a divine word.

"After bringing the rabbi home to his worried family, the abbot heads back toward the monastery finding himself haunted by the unyielding conviction of this no-nonsense man whom he knew to be an even scholar never given to flights of religious fancy. By the time he arrives home, some small part of the abbot has been captured by the rabbi's dream. He neither believes nor disbelieves it. He tells the story to the other monks flatly, by way of sharing the days events over a meal. As he tells it, he cannot help but look into their eyes—the same eyes he has looked into a thousand times—and ask himself, 'What if . . . ? what if . . . ?'

"As the days pass by, all the monks find that the rabbi's dream haunts them as well. They look at each other and ask, 'What if . . . ?' And imperceptibly, they find that they are beginning to treat each other more graciously. At first, it is only that they catch each others' eyes more often; then they find themselves offering needless smiles or unnecessary kind words. Soon the sharp edge of their daily life has been softened by something approaching mercy.

"As the months pass by, they find themselves more ready to serve and even defer to one another. They look out for each others' needs and little daily pleasures, a favorite dish carefully prepared, flowers set on the table, a younger hand assisting an older member into his chair. And they neither believe nor disbelieve the rabbi's dream.

"As the years pass by, two things happen in the monastery: first, the rabbi's dream is forgotten; there is no more talk of the Messiah among them. But even though the dream is forgotten, their life together has been imperceptibly transformed. Its day-to-day routines, its prayers, the meals together, daily work, all are lit with a glimmer of kindness and mercy, a bright reflection of grace, all because of a suspicion that they should perhaps regard each other not simply from a human point of view."

After the sermon, I moved from the pulpit to the communion table. There was set a heavenly banquet of Wonder Bread and Welch's grape juice. Over the sticky perfume of the trays of shot-glass cups and cubed white bread, I looked across the table at all the saints. I knew their stories, often I knew more than I wanted to know. "This is the joyful feast of the people of God," I began, a declaration countered by the evidence.

Every year as a part of this day's feast we read the names of those who have passed from this life into the congregation oddly named the Church Triumphant. Then we imagine the truth: that this is a table that stretches into eternity. We rise as the names are read and stand in sober silence for an eternal minute. The list is lately too long for a congregation this small. The third of nine names was "Minnie Berle MacDowell." I looked for Angus in his accustomed pew, saw him with his eyes closed, and would swear that Minnie was standing beside him. I trusted that he would fare well for what time providence might set before him. Nearly a century of stubborn faith had carved a groove in his soul, and that groove would keep him moving, steadily and forward.

I looked at all the faces across the table from me and could not help but ask as I looked at each, *Could this be the one?* None of them were even remotely likely candidates. But it was somebody; somebody had done it. I looked from Bob Beener to Jimmy and Ardis Wilcox. *Hardly,* I mouthed to myself. In the second pew stood Alvina Johnson next to Elma and Carmen Krepke, both in church for the reading of Minnie's name. *Never,* I thought with a quick and cynical shake of my head. I looked to Angus. *No, too tight-fisted and nothing to his name but the house on Monroe and his Social Security check.* I thought of the people I had met from Westminster Church in Elm Forest. Most of them worked in auto plants or the remaining downriver steel mills. A lot of them were on pension. They were hardly flush, and anyway, they didn't really know us that well.

Yet someone had sent a lawyer in Chicago a largish check, and that lawyer had sent me another containing a typed note on a piece of plain white paper that read simply: "This is to help with a house. For a down payment. Pay it back when you can, but only if you can. No interest." The other correspondence, formal and from the attorney, noted the obvious: this benefactor wished to remain anonymous, and all I had to do was sign and return the enclosed document indicating receipt. Any repayment might be made through his office.

The awkward challenge that had faced us in this move was the question of where we would live. Like many small-town ministers, we had lived in a church-owned house in North Haven, generously named a "manse" in Presbyterian tradition. It was not an altogether unhappy arrangement in a town where it is almost impossible to sell a house when you leave. But my new congregation owned no manse, and we had been able to save next to nothing. We had reconciled ourselves to renting.

At first I found the anonymity of the gift maddening. I wanted to know. I resented the way it drove me and Annie to speculation. But oddly, in time the speculation that haunted us was having an unanticipated effect. As I looked into the faces of all the impossible candidates in Minnesota and imagined the equally impossible ones in Michigan, the *Hardly* that I always had found myself muttering, had slowly become *Well, you never know.*

After reading the names of the saints departed, the saints present sat themselves down on their mortal bums. I turned to the feast set before us and said the Words of Institution for this last time in this place. Then I raised the flagon and chalice, pouring the sweet, unfermented fruit of the vine from one to the other. For the first time in my life, I spilled it. I was looking at faces, not what I was doing. I forgot myself and poured too much. My cup overflowed, sticky sweet grape juice running down my arm and robe and onto the white linen cloth covering the table. It struck me funny, this Psalmic image of abundance, but I maintained clerical composure.

I whole broke the loaf set before me for that purpose without incident and took my seat in the single oak minister's chair set behind the table. Along with everybody else, I waited to be served, first the tray with soft, white bread carved that morning into neat half-inch cubes by Ardis Wilcox and Bob Beener's wife, Elaine. Flesh and blood is such a jolting and coarse image, the stuff of mortal being; we have rendered it tidy and easily handled.

Larry Wilcox was one of the four elders serving that morning. He brought the plate of bread to one end of the lone choir pew; they passed it soberly on to the next. Larry retrieved it at the other end of the pew and moved to me. I reached for a cube, pinching it daintily between my index finger and thumb. But as I lifted it off the plate, ten more little cubes followed. This one slice of Wonder Bread had not been cut quite clean through. I shook my chosen piece to dislodge the others, but they held on tenaciously. Suddenly the sequestered emotion of the day burst out in a silent, trembling laughter. Again I shook my piece, again to no avail. And then I laughed in church, as I had not since I was a poorly behaved child. Larry Wilcox watched me, plate in hand. He saw my giggles and started to chortle himself, his shoulders shaking with suppressed mirth. Soon I noticed that most of the congregation was doing the same, not open laughter of course, but something even more fun, hidden, like children hide their giggles from adults. The joyful feast of the people of God. You reach for one little piece of grace and find that you have more on your hands than you deserve or ever imagined you needed.

Center Point Publishing
600 Brooks Road ● PO Box 1
Thorndike ME 04986-0001 USA

(207) 568-3717

US & Canada:
1 800 929-9108